CAST BY THE SEA

THERESA VERBOORT

CAST BY THE SEA

THERESA VERBOORT

TWIST & TURN PRESS
Publishing Services for Indie Authors

CAST BY THE SEA

DEDICATION

This book is dedicated to
my long suffering and supportive husband
and my writer's group which gave me
the courage to publish.

FOREWARD

BANDON is a small town on the southern Oregon coast. While the town is real, it is only the setting of the stories that follow, all of which are figments of the author's imagination. Set in mid-century, the people and places depicted, some very loosely inspired by real characters, are all completely imaginary and any resemblance to persons living or dead is purely coincidental.

TABLE OF CONTENTS

1. Introduction
2. Final Return
3. Lucy's Revenge
4. Fear on the Mountain
5. Reenie's Good Day
6. The Hairdresser
7. A Sailor and His Girl
8. Girls' Rebellion
9. The Ugly Duckling
10. The Town Dog
11. A Life Forgotten
12. The Ranch
13. The Sellars
14. The Girl Who Talked to Birds
15. Tit for Tat
16. Remembering Ella
17. Mrs. Riggert
18. Love and Marriage
19. Violet Gantler
20. Reenie, Her Last Chapter

About the Author

A car, carrying two women,
is wending its way down
the coast highway.

CHAPTER ONE

INTRODUCTION

DRIVING DOWN HIGHWAY 101 through the Coast Mountains south of Coos Bay, the wildness of the area begins to hit you. You see mile after mile of green, mostly cedars, firs, alders and the rank coastal brush. Once in a while you can glimpse a steep, barren hillside, stripped of all its growth by loggers. There are few signs of human habitation until you get closer to town.

You see the place as a quiet little coastal town, strung out along highway 101, clinging to the cliffs along the blue Pacific, slumbering along the banks of the Coquille River. It has changed much over the centuries. In the dim shadows of the past, before man can remember, the spirit of it was here. The river flowed into the sea, unrestricted, the land formed by the winds, tides and eternal pushing of the continental plates against one another. This land has seen earthquakes, tsunamis, floods, ice—all the calamities that beset the earth and shape it.

Thousands of years ago, the No-So-Ma people settled in the region. They were hunters and gatherers, living in small groups along the riverbanks. They used the abundant game,

1

fish and shellfish, wild berries and plants for food. They were excellent weavers and made beautiful baskets. They wore animal skins, and skirts and rain capes made of shredded cattail leaves. They knew the many uses of the herbs and plants of the area. Giant trees and intensely verdant brush and grasses covered the land. The wetlands teemed with fish and birds.

The No-So-Ma traded goods with the other natives of the region. They lived their lives and told their stories. They were not prepared for the devastation to come.

At first, they traded furs with the white men who began invading the area. But as more of them came, they desired the lands of the native peoples. Soon, there was fighting and murder on both sides. The people of the land were overwhelmed by the brutality of the invaders. Eventually, their villages burned to the ground and they were driven by disease and war into settling on reservations. More and more white men came.

By the mid-1850s white settlers were taking over the area. Near the end of that decade, Captain William Rackleff decided that he could get his trading ship over the bar and into the bay of the Coquille River. By the 1860s ships were coming into the dangerous mouth of the river for trading purposes.

In 1873, a supposed Irish "Lord," George Bennett, (the facts of the title are disputed) beheld the area for the first time. He had traveled from Bandon, Ireland with his two sons to find a new world to conquer and make his fortune. The green slopes of the land, the rugged cliffs rising abruptly above the beaches, reminded him of his far away home. So, he purchased a large parcel of it on the bluff overlooking the sea and settled in with his sons. He prospered, and trade and commerce increased in the area. Bandon was named after his hometown in Ireland.

He was homesick for his native land, so he imported plants from home to landscape his grounds. This is how the scourge of the region entered the picture. Gorse, Irish Furze, its beautiful bright yellow blossoms and lushly green stems belying the curse of its piercing, sharp thorns, loved the area. It loved it so much, that it became the ecological terrorist of the town. It marched over the land and cliffs, smothering the local native plants in its path. The salal, huckleberries, ferns, rhododendrons, and azaleas could not hold it back. It rudely shoved them aside and became a militant curse, which nothing could stop. It is nearly indestructible. Dig it up, burn it, sear it with chemicals, and it will eventually grow right back. In the spring, it produces beautiful, brilliant deep-yellow blossoms. In the long, rainless summer months, it becomes as dry as a burnt cookie; its oily branches dry out, exuding an incendiary oil. A spark can set them off. If a fire gets into it, it burns like a dried-up Christmas tree.

In 1878 Bennett convinced the Oregon legislature to fund the construction of the jetties that protect the bar to this day. When they were built, engineers dynamited a picturesque, enormous rock monolith that loomed over the town near the edge of the sea. This was sacred to the No-So-Mah, but that meant little to the white men. The engineers blasted it into gigantic boulders. These were hauled out on train tracks and dumped into the sea, creating a stable bar for the ships to cross.

The natives were incensed at the desecration of their sacred rock. All that was left was an enormous, gaping hole in the cliff sides. The angry No-So-Mah medicine woman, watching the blasting in the distance, placed a curse on the town. She lifted her arms, looked to the heavens, and in a moaning, mournful chant, pronounced that the town would burn three times.

Sternwheelers and sailing vessels plied the waters of the Coquille, carrying off lumber, dairy products, fish and woolen goods. The town flourished. Houses sprang up and businesses and churches. It was a real town. Then, in 1914, the first fire struck. Most of the business district was destroyed. But within a year the area had been rebuilt, and was prospering again. This continued until the second fire struck in 1936.

That hot, dry summer, with extremely low humidity, kept the Coos County Fire Patrol and Civilian Conservation Corps running from one fire to the next. The morning of September 26, Bandon residents were warned that a fire was approaching from the east. At first, the citizens didn't seem overly concerned. They thought the fire would pass them by. But the wind shifted, bringing the fire to the city. The dry gorse took off in an explosion of flame. People fled to the shore, or to boats in the harbor. Many rowed across to the lighthouse on the north shore to escape the flames. The furious fire wiped out the town. When it was all over, few buildings remained.

Gradually, the town struggled back to life. Two of the mills and the International Battery Separator factory had survived and soon re-opened. The high school was still standing and was quickly put back into business with the grade school children placed in the basement and gymnasium. Some people moved away from the area. Those who remained, rebuilt. However, it was no longer the pretty Victorian town it had once been. The new business section consisted of plain, false-fronted western-style buildings. There was no landscaping, no prettifying of the practical replacements. The people must have been discouraged when they saw the cursed gorse come back in the spring, its yellow blossoms waving defiantly in the breeze.

So, the life of the town endured. In the 1940s, 50s, and 60s the lumber business was booming, the fishing industry thrived, as did the cranberry business. The dairies of the area sent their milk to the local creamery, which made splendid cheeses. The few motels were kept afloat by the tourists who came through. The little town was comfortable, if not exciting. So far, it hasn't burned the third time.

But now it's the middle of 2001. The shore birds sailing overhead have passed the message that someone is coming. A car, carrying two women, is wending its way down the coast highway. These are familiar people to the town. They lived here in the mid-twentieth century, a good time to grow up in small town America. Why are they coming? They're bringing someone home.

You can't grow up here without
the rhythms of the sea becoming
part of your body and soul.

CHAPTER TWO

FINAL
RETURN

THE BEIGE TOYOTA VAN wound its way down highway 101 on a sunny fall afternoon. As it left North Bend and followed the edge of the water, Alicia lowered the driver's window, held up her chin and sniffed deeply, then smiled. "Don't you just love the smell of fresh wood chips?" she asked, glancing at her sister, Sophie.

Sophie breathed deeply. "Yeah, it always tells me we're home." She shifted in her seat, tucked her left leg under her knee.

Alicia sighed. "Another twenty miles and we'll be there. I'm glad we have reservations. We can check in and then run down to the beach. We'll get to watch the sunset. That's one of my favorite things to do."

"Sounds great. I haven't been to the beach in months. I miss it." Sophie stretched and yawned, then turned and pulled out the snack bag from behind the seat. "Want a protein bar?"

"Sure, I'm a bit hungry. It's a few hours 'til dinner."

Sophie unwrapped the bar and handed it to Alicia. "That'll hold you until we can eat."

"Thanks, Sis. I love traveling with you. You can read my mind."

"Ha, I wish I could do that. You're usually two steps ahead of me."

Alicia barked a "Ha!" and they sank into amiable silence.

They drove through the downtown Coos Bay traffic, and sped on south on 101. They usually made this pilgrimage about once a year, pulled by the call of the sea and memories of Bandon as it was when they were growing up. They would go to check out the changes, take flowers to their family members' graves, nurse ancient wounds, and remind themselves why they wanted to escape the small-town confines of the place.

However, this time they had a different mission. They were bringing home their mother's ashes to place them in the plot next to their father's grave. She had completed her life at the age of ninety-five. She bought the gravesite when she buried their father in 1977. Even after she moved up to Portland to be near the girls she had held on to the paperwork for that site. Now, 28 years later, this was where she wanted to rest, next to her husband. Alicia had made arrangements with the mortician and the local priest so they could place the container there and have prayers said over it. Alicia glanced back at the box on the back seat. It felt like their mother was sitting there, smiling serenely at the scenery.

They crossed the Coquille River on the "new" bridge. Alicia glanced at Sophie. With her short, dark brown hair and brown eyes, Sophie looked much younger than sixty-five. Even in their "senior" years, she was still the family beauty, with beautiful, clear skin, just a dusting of freckles and a perfect, up-turned nose.

"Remember the old days when we had to cross the river on the ferry? I was always terrified that we'd end up in the water, especially when the river was swollen and bouncing with whitecaps. I'd close my eyes when we eased down to the ferry and grit my teeth all the way across."

Sophie shivered. "Yeah, me too. I'd pray 'Hail Mary's' all the way across the river. I was so relieved when the bridge went up."

"It's funny that I still think of it as the 'new' bridge. It must be over fifty years old by now."

Sophie looked out over the calm water, sparkling in the afternoon sun. "I swear, I used to hold my breath until we drove up the ramp and were on dry land again."

Alicia slowed down as Sophie whipped out her camera, rolled down her window, and snapped photos of the river as they went. They crossed the bridge as a car whizzed past going north. Soon they spied the "Bandon By The Sea" sign, and shouted the words together. Sophie laughed. "We're baaaack."

Back in hometown territory, they noticed new businesses sitting on the north end of town, the higher elevation of the area. Highway 101 swooped around a sharp curve and rushed down the long, steep hill, through the lower part of downtown, and continued up the other side and on south, down the coast.

It was still a small town. The new buildings in the small shopping center were undistinguished and fashioned in the modern, disposable shopping mall mode. Most businesses seemed to be surviving, in spite of the near demise of the area's logging and fishing industries. Some had changed hands and purposes. A service station had become a restaurant, the theatre was now a museum. The growing tourist trade kept it afloat. It had been discovered by some of the rich and famous as a "place to get away from it all." The renowned golf course north of town was a big draw among golfing enthusiasts. Escapees from southern California (according to local suspicions) had built expensive homes along the shoreline of the southwest edge of town. In places they had bulldozed out the ever-present gorse and stuck their dream homes on the hills overlooking the waves. Alicia gave them all a year or two in the blast of the frigid west wind and incessant rain before they packed up and went back to where the sun shines. Later, when they drove around the "beach loop," they could see "for sale" signs in front of several of the houses.

In the 40s, 50s and 60s, when the girls were growing up there, the main businesses huddled along the south bank of the Coquille River, which flowed sullenly through the town and flushed itself out to sea through its narrow mouth, edged by the north and south jetties.

There was a main street, featuring the one clothing store in town, a drugstore, a couple of pubs, the local newspaper, and small businesses, which stopped after a few blocks and, turned by a weed patch, veered and went for a block down to the cross street along the river. Here, you could go right, and follow the river up past a few business buildings, including the seafood processing plant and docks, then past the huge Moore Mill, the main employer of the town, which squatted out over the river on battered piers. A dreary gray place, the mill teemed with workers and machinery, surrounded by huge piles of logs and stacks of lumber. Townies always knew when the workers went to lunch, or their shift was over, by the screaming of the loud mill whistle.

If you chose to go left at the intersection of Main and South River Street, you would follow the river on out past a few small, wind-blown houses, past the two-story Coast Guard Station, (sparkling white with dark green shutters, the handsomest building downtown), and on out to the south jetty. Here you could park and watch the wind and waves batter the stout jetties and the abandoned lighthouse on the north bank of the river.

Residents consider this the most scenic beach in Oregon. Alicia still agreed with that sentiment. The surf breaks over huge, monolithic pillars and blocks of stone, which march down the beach for miles. The roar of the surf as it sprays over these gigantic monuments of nature, dramatically flinging huge plumes of foamy salt water into the air, mesmerizes the observer. One could sit for hours, sheltered from the wind by a friendly outcropping, immersed in the sounds and sights and scents of it all. You can't grow up here without the rhythms of the sea becoming part of your body and soul. The first whiff of salt air always lifts your heart as you approach the beach.

Those days, the town had no public swimming pool or recreational facility, but it did have a small, one-room public library, Alicia's sanctuary and unguided source of reading materials, attached to the city hall. Also, there was a soda parlor, where one could get sweet treats and hamburgers and schmooze with the other kids, if you had the money, which Alicia and Sophie never did. Also, there was a movie theater, Alicia's favorite place to go on the rare occasions when she had the chance. In the summer they could swim in Bradley Lake, a small lake south of town, nestled in the dunes, or Floras Lake, further south, or in one of the wild streams that flowed through the area.

On the upper, southern end of town, stood the schools and a handful of businesses, including a hamburger joint (which later became the Laughing Gull Cafe) along highway 101.

The main industries of town were lumber and fishing, but the ruby-red cranberry bogs brought added income to the area. A number of small dairies supplied the local creamery, famous for its wonderful cheeses, and provided a steady source of employment for some of the citizens.

Often, Alicia thought it was a dreary place to grow up. It seemed that the cold west wind never quit tearing at the town. She'd have sworn that it rained nine months of the year. The summer and fall dry seasons were sometimes darkened by the gray fog that rolled in from the sea in the late afternoon. Conversely, the dry season brought sun to the area, but it also brought the concern about the dreaded forest fires.

She'd felt isolated from the rest of the world. In the days, before cable, the few TV sets in town received only black and white snow. The chief source of information and news was the radio, newspapers, movie news reels, and, of course Life Magazine, her favorite window to the world "out there."

As a youngster, she was vaguely aware of the Korean War, but it hadn't affected her much. Later in the 50s, the teenagers ignored the Cold War, except for one ridiculous propaganda movie, shown at school, about what to do in case of nuclear attack. "Stay indoors, drink only your melted ice cubes, keep water on hand in your refrigerator," the announcer solemnly proclaimed. It made good fodder for adolescent humor. And, of course, they all hated the "Commies." But always, deep down, in the 50s, lurked the buried fear that they would all be "nuked" into Kingdom Come. Many of the schools had nuclear attack drills, when the students had to hide under their desks. As if that would do any good. Sadly, Alicia reflected upon that. These days, the kids had to have "active shooter" drills. How horrible was that! Humans had not advanced much.

It was a typical ingrown small community. From Alicia's point of view, if you were a "newcomer," (anyone who had moved there since the fire), you were viewed with some suspicion. You had to earn the community's respect. The old-timers and wealthy were the social elite and pretty much ignored you. Their kids ignored your kids too. It took time to become integrated into the community. But the people would stand by each other in an emergency. They looked out for their neighbors. And everyone knew everyone else's business.

The population was 100 percent Caucasian. Oh, there was one olive-skinned Italian, who owned a market in town and gave candy to all the kids at Christmas. But she never saw another non-white face. Thus, the issue of race never came up. However, they did have a rather sizable influx of "Okies" and "Arkies" to look down upon. This allowed the residents to feel superior to their uncouth ways. They laughed at their hick southern accents. Some locals were sure they were stealing their jobs, working for less than anybody else, and thus resented them.

Alicia and Sophie's family lived down the road from some of them and made friends with their kids. One family lived in a converted chicken coop. Another built a wood house with tar paper siding, no sheetrock on the inside. Alicia was impressed by how the mothers managed to make their rustic houses look so cozy and neat and homey, even though they didn't have much. They made pretty curtains for the windows, and covered the bare, plank floors with braided rugs. Their houses were clean and neat and she liked visiting them. They were hard-working and friendly people. But she still sometimes called them "Okies" behind their backs.

Alicia broke the silence. "Remember how important football was to the town when we were growing up? It seemed like the only thing that really mattered was the status of the football team."

Sophie rolled her eyes. "Yeah, football was king. The players could do no wrong."

"Right, if one of them got a girl pregnant, the girl left school in shame and 'disappeared' for a few months. That took care of the problem. The guy went on as usual."

"I remember that the players could come to practice hungover, and the coach could too, but as long as they won games, they were okay." Sophie shook her head. "It used to really bug me."

Alicia was lost in thought. She hadn't been involved or interested in the sport but paid homage to it anyway. Everyone went to the games and cheered wildly. Besides it was something to do on Friday nights.

Alicia glanced at Sophie, who was scrunched down in her seat, looking out the window. "I remember," Sophie said softly. "I kind of liked the games. I felt more like one of the school crowd at the games. In school I usually felt like an outcast."

Yes, Alicia thought, the other girls were jealous and you were so shy that you did everything alone. It must have been miserable. Unfortunately, by the time Sophie was in high school, Alicia was off to college and couldn't help her.

They had grown up distinctly disadvantaged. Not only was their family new to the community, but they'd lived ten miles from town, surrounded by woods. And they were poor. They rode the bus to school. They took sack lunches. They lived with no indoor plumbing, no running water, an outdoor privy—facts that Alicia diligently tried to hide from her classmates. Even worse, they had no telephone. Once they left school for the day, they had no contact with their classmates until the next day.

Growing up in the woods, the town, in spite of its smallness, was a magnet to Alicia. All she wanted to do was go there and be with other kids her age. She watched the behavior of the town kids and tried to be like them. She couldn't afford to keep up with the clothing fads of the day but wore the clothes her loving mother made for her (for which she was forever grateful) and the hand-me-downs from relatives. She took pride in her appearance as best she could. She had a small group of nerdy friends, hardworking students, artsy, who weren't into sports, to run around with.

She hungered for people. She wanted to learn their stories and feel the communion of humanity. She spent as much time as she could, hanging out in town, staying overnight with her best friend, going to school functions.

She had a strong affection for the outcasts and characters of the town. She kept their stories stored in her heart. She watched as they went about their solitary ways, feeling a kinship with them. Sometimes they would pass one of them when riding through town on the school bus. She always wondered where he or she was going. Every town has its odd or "different" people, and their town had more than its share.

CHAPTER THREE

LUCY'S REVENGE

THE VAN SPED AROUND THE CURVE of 101 and on down the hill into the town. Alicia felt a deep twinge of anger as they drove by the empty lot where the creamery had stood. No more of the famous cheeses would be coming out of Bandon. A big conglomerate from the north had bought the business, fired the employees, and razed the building. She averted her eyes as they drove past. They proceeded up the hill on the south end of town and pulled into the parking lot of the Sea View Motel. It was perched on the hillside above old town and had a wonderful, sweeping view of the harbor and the river, all the way out to the ocean. Alicia parked the van and turned to Sophie. "This is my favorite place to stay here. We can see the harbor and all the way out to the ocean."

Sophie nodded her head vigorously. "I love it too. Come on, let's get in there." She opened the door and hopped out.

They checked in and dragged their luggage upstairs. Alicia carefully set the box of ashes on the table by the window. Then she pulled open the drapes to drink in the view. The river and the sea never changed. She was home. She looked down on the street. From here, she could see shops, a pub, and, at the end of the street, a small restaurant. She smiled. "Remember old Mabel?" she mused.

Sophie laughed. "Don't remind me. Thank God, I never tried to work for her. Your experience was enough to scare me off."

Alicia hadn't thought about Mabel in a long time. She suspected that, in her day, Mabel was one of the most disliked women in town. She was the owner and chief cook of the small diner down below. It was The Harbor Cafe then. She was a pretty good cook, (and her customers liked her food, which kept her in business), but an angry, bitter woman. Notorious for firing her help, she nevertheless had a steady supply of fodder for her venomous temper. There were precious few opportunities for employment in the area for women, so applicants kept coming to apply for the waitress jobs, in spite of her reputation. When Alicia applied during her junior year of high school, she thought, "*Well, I get along nicely with people. Surely, she can't be as bad as they say. I'll bet that I can work around her. Maybe others just didn't try hard enough.*" And she stepped innocently into the spider's web.

The first few days, Alicia worked hard, trying to please the old harridan. When she was told to save the unused pats of butter off of the butter dishes of the customers, and add extra water to the orange juice, she reluctantly followed her instructions. When Mabel crabbed at her to hurry up and do the dishes, or mop the floors, or serve the customers, she did her best to comply. But then, Petey, Mabel's homely little bantam of a husband, began showing up to "help" for the day. Petey fancied himself a ladies' man and never missed an opportunity to smile and make small talk with the waitresses. Mabel, who was insanely jealous of her balding little Romeo, immediately began to make the object of Petey's attention as miserable as possible. Eventually, she would find an excuse to fire her. Petey began making excuses to chat Alicia up. She lasted two weeks.

It never occurred to Mabel that any of the normally submissive girls she hired would ever stand up to her. But when she hired a husky girl named Lucy, daughter of one of the local loggers, she met her match. Lucy stoically took all the taunting and complaining that Mabel dished out for six months, a record for Mabel's employees. People in town were taking bets on how long she would last.

Lucy just kept on doing her job, ignoring Petey's toothy interest in her, and avoiding Mabel as much as possible. But one afternoon, after Lucy loaded the dishwasher and turned it on, Mabel exploded one time too many.

"Why did you do that?" she screamed. "There's plenty room for more dishes in there. Are you a total idiot? Do you think I'm made of money, that I can afford to run the dishwasher every time we get a few dishes dirty? What's wrong with you?"

Lucy watched her impassively, her mouth turned down firmly in grim endurance. But Mabel kept berating the girl. Lucy stared at her. When Mabel stopped to take a breath, Lucy spoke up calmly.

"Mabel, you are a mean, cantankerous, vicious old woman and this is my last shift here. After tonight, I won't be back."

"Good," shouted Mabel. "You never could handle the job anyway." She stormed over to her griddle and slapped a steak on it.

Lucy walked into the little cubbyhole where the buckets, mops and brooms were kept, next to the unscrubbed toilet. Her coat and purse hung on a nail in the wall there. She quickly slipped two large boxes of "Ex-lax" she had purchased earlier that day, to take home for her parents, into her apron pocket. She went back out to the front counter and calmly went on serving customers. She kept an eye on the kitchen area, and when she saw Mabel slip out the back door to cool off for a moment with Petey, she stealthily walked back into the kitchen.

Mabel had made a large pot of chocolate pudding that afternoon, and it was sitting on the counter, still hot. Lucy quickly emptied all the Ex-lax into the pot and stirred it until it melted and disappeared into the pudding. She began to dish up the pudding into serving bowls and set them into the cooler. Just about then, Mabel came back in.

"What are you doing?" she snapped. "You're supposed to be waiting out front, not back here messing in my food."

"You know what, Mabel?" retorted Lucy, "I'm not going to finish out my shift after all. I was just trying to give you a hand and all you can do is yell at me. I'm out of here right now and let's just see if you can run this stinkin' place by yourself. You can mail me my check, you old Bitch."

"Good, I don't need you," yelled Mabel. "I have Petey here to help me and he's all I need. Don't know why I ever hired you in the first place."

Mabel and Petey managed to get through the rush hour by themselves. The pudding went over big, and she sold most of it. They decided to close early, since they were shorthanded and she put the tattered "help wanted" sign in the window.

There were a couple of bowls of pudding left over, so Mabel and Petey helped themselves before they went home. As she handed Petey his serving, she smiled smugly. "We earned this, don't you think?"

The next day, about ten of the restaurant's customers came down with a mysterious case of the "runs." They couldn't figure out what was wrong. Some of them called doctor Maxwell, the town's only GP, with their complaints. Alicia could picture him, as he questioned them and began to see a pattern. They had all eaten at Mabel's restaurant. The Doc was privy to the town's secrets, being the only doctor within twenty miles. He'd heard about Mabel. He called her. She and Petey were home in bed with the "flu."

"Mabel, what was on the menu last night at your place?" he asked.

"Why do you want to know?" she gasped, as she doubled over with cramps.

"Well, I think you have a problem down there. I'm going to have to notify the county health department about this outbreak of diarrhea. It seems to be stemming from something you and your customers ate at your place."

"You can't do this," howled Mabel. "You'll put me out of business. What if people hear about this? I run a clean establishment. There's nothing wrong with my food."

"Sorry, Mabel, but I have to do my duty and let the county know. What if this is a serious outbreak? Don't you open the place up until we get to the bottom of this." He hung up the phone and chuckled to himself. He knew Mabel's dark side and how she treated her girls. It was time she got her comeuppance. He called the health department.

The next day, health department inspectors came in to the restaurant, certain that they were onto something big.

They looked over the place from top to bottom. As they did so, they kept checking off violations and problem areas. By the time they were finished, Mabel was handed a three-page list of things to change, clean or fix, before she could open back up. She objected loudly and volubly. But she may as well have been speaking to one of her steel pots.

It cost her $3,500 dollars to replace the peeling linoleum, scratched countertops, and clean out the toilet and sink areas. She also had to have the entire dining area scoured from top to bottom with disinfectant. All the food on hand had to be thrown out and the place fumigated for cockroaches. She was closed down for three weeks. All in all, she figured it cost her $4,500 in repairs and lost business. She never got over it until the day she died.

And Lucy? Well a lot of money changed hands when she quit, as the townspeople collected on their bets. Later on, she got a job at the Laughing Gull Cafe where Alicia worked. They eventually exchanged "Mabel stories," after Lucy swore Alicia to secrecy. They were great friends for years after that.

CHAPTER FOUR

FEAR ON
THE MOUNTAIN

ALICIA AND SOPHIE UNPACKED their suitcases and left the room for the beach. They took the familiar drive past the coast guard station, on around the corner and down to the south jetty. There, they parked and sat watching the waves washing over the ends of the jetties. They watched a bit, mesmerized, as the sun began to lower itself into the sea. They finally got out and walked up on top of the jetty, watching the golden trail of the sun across the water. There were a few clouds on the horizon so the sunset turned into brilliant oranges and purples, searing the sky, while a blinding flare of golden light glistened a path to the shore. Gradually the light diminished until they could no longer see the brilliant ball, only the pale aftermath of light on the horizon. They drove back downtown and cruised Main Street. The town was quiet now that the peak of the tourist season was over. Alicia parked in front of the cafe that had been Mabel's. It was now called The New Wave Cafe these days.

After a tasty fresh fish dinner, they didn't see much to do downtown, so returned to their room. They settled in for an

23

early night, after a couple of hours of TV. As Alicia lay back, she reviewed the day. The drive down had been beautiful, a perfect fall day. *Mom would have loved it,* she thought. She pictured the road, past the magnificent seashore, on through the forested drive from Coos Bay. She was wistful about the loss of the fire lookout on Beaver Hill as they passed the spot where it had once stood. The Coos County Forest Service tore it down, years back.

Alicia had loved working for the forest service. It was her first job right out of high school. At seventeen she had manned a lookout station for the summer, watching for fires. She went through training at the Forest Service headquarters with the other women (there weren't any men in the group). She learned how to use the fire finder, using landmarks to zero in on the location of any smoke. and learned to use the short-wave radios that were the communication system for all the lookouts.

Her first lookout was on top of a bald mountain southeast of Bandon called "Bill's Butte." Her one-room aerie was an old building with four glass walls from ceiling to the bottom 2½ feet or so of walls. It sat directly on the ground, no tower. It was furnished with an iron cot, an old, rusting wood cook stove, table and chair, and the radio stand that held the short-wave radio. Two of the low walls were lined with storage benches for her supplies. The fire-finder stood in the center, with its topographical map and sighting device. This was her living and working quarters. It had a magnificent view to the north, south, and west all the way to the ocean. To the east, the view was blocked by the bulk of coast range mountains, a series of green to blue ridges. She was totally alone until she signed on the short-wave radio in the morning and let headquarters know she was on the job. The radio made a steady stream of static all day until she signed off at night. The noise bothered her at first until she got used to it. Whenever there was a fire, or a lookout needed something, she could follow it over the radio. Every hour, while she was on the air, the dispatcher checked in with all the lookouts to be sure all was well. If she didn't answer, unless she had informed them that she would be out of earshot for a time, they would check back every fifteen minutes until she replied. After four checks, a ranger was dispatched to find out what was wrong. She was always careful not to let that happen.

It was her first room to herself and she loved it. Having grown up in a tiny house that held eight people, sharing a bed with her sisters, she relished the privacy and the quiet. She felt quite grown up and independent. She even enjoyed chopping wood for the stove. The silence of the place didn't bother her. She had grown up in the woods, and found it peaceful. She had a little portable radio when she wanted the sound of a human voice. And the static on the short wave was frequently interrupted by fire patrol business. She wasn't worried about safety because a locked gate blocked the gravel road leading up to the lookout. Besides, she had her mongrel dog, Blondie, and her gun, a .22-gauge rifle. Her father made sure she knew how to use it before she set out on her new adventure.

Once a week her parents brought her up fresh supplies and books. The forest patrol brought up water in large thirty-gallon milk cans regularly. She was frugal with it, and used a wash pan for her daily ablutions. The toilet was an old outhouse a short distance down and across the road that led to her summer home. It spooked her terribly when she first looked into it. It was festooned with spider webs. But once she swept it out managed to use it without worry.

She did a good job that first summer and was rewarded the second summer by being the first one to inhabit the brand-new tower built on Beaver Hill. This one had electricity, an electric stove and lights. It sat four stories high on top of Beaver Hill, overlooking the Coquille Valley to the east and forested hills to the north, south and, to the west all the way to the blue of the sea.

Here, she hauled her own water up the steps in buckets. Her water source was a boxed-in spring across the road from the lookout and down the hillside, with a narrow path through the greenery. It was a pleasant place to fill her buckets, with the surrounding trees and ferns giving it a grotto-like effect. Blondie loved to go to the spring with her. The tower was confining and she had to be let out several times a day to go for a run and do her business. She always came back.

The Forest Service encouraged its lookout personnel to invite the public in to see how the operation worked. Since the tower was near a fairly well-traveled gravel county road, she had occasional visitors. Some people were merely curious, others wanted to check her map for good places to pick berries or wild edibles. One day, a man asked to come up to look at the map on the fire finder. He claimed he was looking for places to hunt mushrooms. Alicia let him up, showed him the map, and they chatted a little. He was youngish, wearing jeans and a flannel shirt, with a few days' growth of whiskers on his face. He told her his name, Allen Trotter, looking at her expectantly. She told him that she was Alicia but didn't give him her last name. He asked her where she went to school and where she was from. She was uncomfortable with all the questions and gave him short answers. He checked out the map, and asked her a few questions about the roads in the area. Then he asked her if she was ever allowed to leave to visit with friends.

This made her more uneasy. She realized that she was alone with a strange man and edged around to be in reach of her gun, hidden under her cot. He seemed to be lingering for no reason. "Sometimes, if I'm fogged in and can't see anything, I go home in town for a shower and to pick up supplies and see my family. That's about it."

The radio crackled and started roll call for the hourly check-in. "Um, I have to answer that. I'll let you back down now so I can attend to my work." He slowly ambled on out the door and climbed down the steps as she let down the hatch and locked it. The incident left her unsettled.

Three nights later, she was sound asleep when something woke her with a start. The tower was vibrating. It always vibrated when there was a strong wind or someone was coming up the steps. She waited. She noticed that Blondie was sitting up, her ears alert. She let out a low whine. It wasn't the wind. Yes, there was definitely someone climbing up the stairs. As she lay there, the vibrations continued, slowly, stealthily. She felt a shiver of fear flash down her spine as her arms were covered with goosebumps.

Alicia slipped out of bed and padded over to the radio. She turned it on, reassured by the static that streamed out, and quietly told the night dispatcher that she had an intruder. "Are you locked in for the night?"

"Yes. I was sound asleep but someone's coming up my stairs."

"Don't confront him. I'll notify the state police. They should be there shortly."

"Okay. I'm leaving the radio on until I figure out what's going on."

She pulled her rifle out from under her bed and sat there, waiting. The intruder kept climbing. There was nothing for it but to check it out. Quietly, she slipped out the door, her bare feet registered the cold, wet deck and she shivered. Blondie padded out behind her. Shivering in the cold, she stood near the hatch, listened while someone stealthily tried to push it open. Blondie started to bark and growl. The intruder couldn't budge the heavy thing, of course. Blondie snarled again, just as Alicia yelled, "Who's there? I have a gun and I'll use it if I have to."

She recognized the man's voice immediately. The mushroom hunter. He yelped, "Don't shoot, it's me, Allen. I was just wanting to come up for a visit. Can you open the hatch?"

"Of course not. It's the middle of the night. What were you thinking? You can't come up, so leave."

"Awe, I don't mean no harm. I just was lonely and thought you might like some company."

"Go away. Now."

"I brought a bottle of wine. Thought you might like a sip." He reached his hand around the deck and made as if to climb out over the railing. She yelped and smashed the butt of the rifle on his hand. He roared and jerked back and began stumbling down the steps. She heard the bottle crash on the ground far below. "You don't have to be so mean. I just wanted to visit, Bitch. You'll be sorry for this."

Alicia fired her rifle into the ground, to let him know she meant business, and watched while he fled, cursing, on down the stairs. As he scrambled for his car, she fired again. He put on a burst of speed, jumped into his vehicle, and, peeled out of the driveway, throwing gravel as he went.

Shaking, she went back inside and called the dispatcher. She let him know what had happened and he told her to wait up until the police showed up. When the police finally came, with lights flashing and tires squealing to a stop, she let them up and told them what had happened. They took down a description of the culprit, and she told them the make and color of his rusty old pickup. They took off after him.

Having calmed down, she explained what had happened to the dispatcher and said that she was going back to bed. The dispatcher thanked her, expressing his relief. She thanked the dispatcher for calling the police and logged off for the night. However, she didn't get much sleep the rest of the night. She had never felt threatened like that before. It was unnerving.

The next morning, she was informed that the police had chased down the man and arrested him. He was passed out, drunk, and, after looking into his record, they discovered that he had just been released from prison after serving time for an assault conviction. He went back to prison.

Alicia smiled to herself as she relived the incident. She had felt very empowered that night, having defended herself and handled the situation. Snuggling down, she drifted off to sleep.

She relived his last moments,
as he slogged through the
heat and mud right into
a firefight.

CHAPTER FIVE

REENIE'S GOOD DAY

THE NEXT MORNING Allie and Sophie went out to the Laughing Gull for breakfast. As they entered the place, a wave of nostalgia hit Allie. "Remember Reenie, the little lady who used to cook here? She was here when I worked here my junior and senior years. She was a character."

Sophie laughed. "She was a town legend. Small but mighty. And when she worked here the staff was always laughing."

"True. She knew all the gossip about everybody in town. Of lot of the locals ate here. She was a crack-up." Allie giggled. "She told me once that she drove for fifteen years before she finally went in and got her license."

"That's hysterical," Sophie laughed.

"She told me that half the women in town drove without licenses in the 40s and 50s. She finally got scared into getting one by old skanky Mel. Remember him? The deputy who was always handing out traffic tickets? Anyway, she thought he was watching her too closely so she decided to go legal.

Sophie cackled. Mel had terrorized the town denizens who teetered on the edge of law-breaking. There was nothing he loved more than handing out tickets.

"She passed her driver's exam with flying colors, and the examiner said, 'My, you drive like you've been driving for years. Amazing, considering that you've only practiced for three weeks.'"

"Reenie just smiled sweetly and told him, 'Oh yes! I'm a really fast learner. And I've watched my husband drive for years.' She got her license."

When the waitress brought the menus to their booth Allie asked her, "Did you know Reenie?"

"Land, yes. She was a fixture here. Everybody loved her. Did you know her?"

"Yes. I worked with her when I was in school."

"Yeah? She passed away a few years back. She had one of the biggest funerals we've ever had here. Filled the church. People getting up and telling stories about her. My Dad told me that she befriended him when he was in school here. He used to go in there for a coke after school. She'd talk to him. She knew that his Dad had skipped out on the family, that his Mom was kind of absent, mentally. When he was in Vietnam, she wrote to him every week. Those were the only letters he got the whole time he was there. He loved her." Pause. "You two decide what you want while I bring you drinks. Coffee?"

"For sure. And we both take cream." Allie stared dreamily out the window. "Reenie and Mom were good friends. The two of them used to have the best time together."

Sophie glanced over her menu. "Was her real name 'Reenie'?"

"It was actually Irene. But she didn't like it and her little brother could only pronounce 'Reenie.' So, the nickname stuck. I just loved her. She was a boundless bundle of energy, and ran the kitchen like clockwork. Remember how tiny she was? She wore her hair in a bun on top of her head to make herself look taller. Whenever she was around, there was lots of laughter as she joshed with the staff. And she made sure that the waitresses brought her all the latest gossip. They heard it all. Remember Annie? That tall, curvy redhead that all the men panted over, even though she was married? She was especially good at getting all the gossip out of the locals. Reenie asked her once how she found out so much and she said, 'If I want to know somethin', I just ask'em. They love to blab.'" They both chuckled.

They both placed their breakfast order, then lifted their coffee cups and drank a toast to Reenie.

REENIE

Annie and Reenie couldn't have been more different. Little Reenie was helping her husband raise one hulking son and two adventurous daughters. When she wasn't working at the restaurant, she was working at home. She kept a tight rein on her children and marched the whole family to church every Sunday.

Annie was married to a slick character, Rick Cummins, who cheated on her but always managed to sweet talk her back when she found out about his escapades.

She would cry on Reenie's shoulder with each episode and then fall right back under his spell. Reenie kept advising her to leave the bum but she never did. She'd say, "He promised it would never happen again. What can I do? I love him. Besides, the girls need their Dad."

Reenie despised Rick, pure and simple. He was good-looking and sold real estate around town. Reenie was so fed up with the way he yanked Annie around, she vowed she'd fix his wagon someday.

One day, her day off, she needed to take Robbie, her boy, a lunch that he had forgotten. She couldn't stand to think of him going hungry. He was working that summer with a county road crew, and they were miles from town. She turned off the main road onto what she thought was the road where they were clearing brush, but soon realized that it was a fire road that led nowhere. She was looking for a place to turn around and came across Rick's car, parked in a clearing beside the road. She looked in and there he was, with that niece of Joyce Maynard's, who was visiting that summer. That girl was only fifteen if she was a day. It made her blood boil. She stopped her car, walked over and jerked the door open. They both jumped and Rick nearly fell out of the car. She leaned in and yelled at him. "You son of a bitch!"

She glared at the girl. "Lila-Mae, you get your shirt on and get your sweet ass into my car this minute. I'm taking you back to your aunt's place right now."

The girl looked mutinous and started to speak, but Reenie stuck her face in further and said, "You get in my car, missy. I won't tell on you this time, but you better not pull this again. This here is a married man, and you've no business fooling with him." Lila Mae glared at Reenie but slid out of the car, slammed the door behind her, and flounced over to Reenie's car.

Reenie turned on Rick next. "If I ever see or hear of you fooling around on Annie again I'll go straight to the police.

That girl can't be more than fifteen. What you were about to do is statutory rape and I'll see that everyone in town knows about it, including the chief. Don't you ever, ever hurt Annie again or I'll put your feet to the fire. Furthermore, I hear that Lila Mae's father is a cop up in Eugene, and he isn't goin' to take kindly to a grown man fooling around with his little girl. You got that?"

He turned pale, squirmed in his seat. "She told me that she was eighteen, I didn't know. We didn't do anything. Just foolin' around."

"You're a rotten liar and a philanderer and your days of tomcattin' around had better be over."

She turned around and left, took Robbie his lunch and deposited the girl back at her aunt's. Lila Mae returned home two days later. And Annie never cried about Rick's extramarital flings again.

It was a cold day in March 1969. Reenie stared out the big, plate-glass windows in the front of the restaurant. She was slumped on one of the stools at the counter, taking a well-earned break from the kitchen in the afternoon lull before school let out. Her thoughts were as gloomy as the eternally gray January skies, weeping incessantly outside, the rain blown fiercely sideways by the ever-present wind. The gusts frequently slammed the window with sheets of water. Her coffee grew as cold as her mood while she sank into the sorrow that always lurked just beneath her surface.

Her mood shifted as she relived what had happened that morning when she came to work. As she unlocked the door, she thought she heard the faint sound of a child crying. She looked around but saw no one, so pushed on into the restaurant. As she began her preparations for the breakfast crowd, she could still hear the heartrending sound. Where was it coming from? Worried, she went back outside and looked around the building. As she approached the telephone booth in front of the building, the sound grew louder. She peered through the glass. There was a tiny boy, no more than three, sobbing, trapped inside. She hastily pushed in the door and drew him to her. He had bright red curls, and had obviously dressed himself. His shirt was inside out and backwards, his trousers haphazardly fastened. No socks. Untied tennis shoes. He was wearing a light windbreaker. His crying dissolved into gulping sobs.

Reenie knelt in front of the red-faced boy and wiped his face with her apron. "There, there. You're okay now. How did you end up here, child? What's your name? Where are your parents?"

"Bertie," he gulped. "I want my mommy and daddy."

Reenie smiled and tried to calm him. "It's okay, Sweetie. We'll find them. Why don't you come with me, Bertie? I know where there's some hot chocolate. And then maybe we can find your folks. Okay?"

He nodded, his shaking subsiding as she led him into the warmth of the restaurant. "Now, you just sit here, Bertie, in this nice, comfy booth, and I'll get you some yummy hot chocolate."

He looked hopeful when she mentioned hot chocolate again, a smile tentatively twitching his tear-stained face. She hastily heated up the hot chocolate, adding a big dollop of whipped cream, and brought it to him. He immediately settled down with a happy "Oh" at the sight of the treat. He swiped a finger through the whipped cream and licked it.

Reenie grabbed the phone and called the police station. Big Al Picked it up.

"Al, it's Reenie. I have a stray child here at the restaurant. Would you like to come and collect him?"

"Be right there. Haven't had a report on any missing kids. What's he look like?"

"Looks to be about three and has bright red hair. Very cute."

"Oh, I know who that is. I've had to take him home before. I'll be right up. Don't let him get away."

"I won't let him out of my sight. It's a wonder he wasn't run over. See you soon."

Big Al showed up ten minutes later. He filled the doorway as he entered the place. He loomed over the child, hands on hips. "Well, Bertie, you did it again, didn't you? You're in trouble now, Boy." Bertie didn't look impressed. He smiled up at Big Al.

"I want to go play. Mommy and Daddy sleeping."

Big Al turned towards Reenie. "Where'd you find him?"

"He was stuck in the phone booth and couldn't get out. It's a good thing he was, or he might've got out on the highway and been run over. Scared me to death."

"He's done this before. Gets up before the rest of the household and just takes off. They don't seem to have enough sense to put a lock on the door that he can't reach. I'll take him home. Thanks, Reenie."

"Thank God you know where he comes from. I was worried something had happened to his parents."

"No. They're just not too bright. Shouldn't be havin' kids, if you know what I mean."

Reenie watched them go, the child's tiny hand curled in Big Al's ham sized one. As she watched them leave, she was thinking that it was a crime that people didn't cherish and protect their children more. Such a precious boy. Precious as her Robbie.

As she rested there, Reenie's mind went far away, to Vietnam with her boy. She relived his last moments, as he slogged through the heat and mud right into a firefight. One of his buddies had written her a letter from his hospital bed, after it happened. He told her how bravely her darling Robbie had fought, tried to help the wounded, before he was finally shot down. "Your son is a hero. He saved my life and many others." She had wept over the letter. But the post-humous purple heart was no comfort.

She was grateful they'd recovered his body. The military funeral had been true to the military code, formal and stiff. They fired a rifle salute, and she flinched at the sounds as if they had been aimed at her, before they handed her the folded flag. She hugged it tightly, as the pain shot through her. Gerry put his arm around her as tears trickled down his cheeks. But there wasn't any comfort for either of them. They would never get over the loss of their only son.

The girls graduated from high school. Audrey went to the University of Oregon while Molly went to Monmouth. Their home was an empty place these days. She was glad she could still work. It helped pass the time. Gerry would retire in a year or two, but she didn't want to yet. How else would she fill the hours? You can do only so much crocheting and volunteering with the Altar Society. She wasn't a club joiner.

She looked at the big clock on the wall behind the counter. School would be out soon. The high school kids would be piling in to get their burgers and fries and cokes.

She sighed, and went back to the kitchen to see if everything was ready for the onslaught.

They were busy for an hour or so after school let out. Reenie enjoyed seeing the kids come and go. She knew most of them by name and sometimes they joshed back and forth. Then things slacked off a bit. Into the quiet that fell before the dinner rush, the door tinkled as a customer walked in.

Reenie heard Jen, the waitress, exclaim, "Well, hello, Sweetheart, what can we do for you?"

Curious, she peeked out the order window and couldn't see anyone, so she popped out to the front and looked over the counter. There stood a small, skinny girl, no more than eight or ten, looking cold and nervous. She was wearing a cotton dress and tennis shoes. Her jacket was rather dirty, her eyes worried. Her unwashed hair was pulled back into a careless ponytail. She held out her hand and displayed a quarter plus small change. Her voice quavered, "What can I buy for this?"

"Why, Honey, you can getta ice cream cone."

The girl ducked her head. "How much does a hamburger cost?"

"I'm afraid that's seventy-five cents, Sweetie."

Sadly, the girl nodded. "Okay, I guess I'll have a ice cream cone then."

Reenie spoke up. "Aren't you the Bidwell girl? I've seen you walking by here before."

The girl nodded.

"Well now, you know what? I don't think Jen, here, knew about the special we're having for the next twenty minutes. I happen to know that for 35¢ you can get a hamburger, fries and a milkshake. You just sit down here at the counter and

I'll get them for you in a jiffy. Jen, you get her a milkshake while I cook up the rest."

Jen, eyebrows raised, shot Reenie an exasperated look. Before she could say anything, Reenie trotted back into the kitchen and slapped a burger on the grill, then popped the potatoes into the fryer. She had recognized the child, and knew more than Jen about her home life. The kid needed a decent meal for sure. She'd take the money to cover it out of the tip jar.

She watched with satisfaction as the child's eyes grew huge at the sight of the meal set before her. She immediately began to wolf down the food.

"Take your time, Sweetie. It's not going to run away. What's your name, Honey?"

"Brenda." She ducked her head.

"Well, Brenda, you come see me anytime, you hear? I have lots of specials."

The girl eyed her gratefully, her cheeks full, and nodded. She managed a shy, muffled, "Thank you." Reenie kept her eye on her until she finished every last crumb of her food and left.

Well, Reenie thought, I guess this has been a good day after all. At least two kids were better off because of her. She smiled to herself as she went back into the kitchen, greeted the night cook, and hung up her apron. Her feet hurt, her back ached, and she was bone tired. But her shift was over, and she was going home to Gerry.

CHAPTER SIX

THE
HAIRDRESSER

AFTER BREAKFAST, Allie and Sophie drove over to the funeral home, where the town undertaker, John Hauser, called the priest, Father Omolo, who was expecting to hear from them. They agreed to go directly to the cemetery and bury their mother's urn in her plot.

"I've arranged to have the dates chiseled on our parent's double headstone, so that should be ready for us to check out," Allie explained.

Hauser nodded. "It's all done. I think you'll like it."

They drove back north through town towards the small Catholic cemetery, where they would meet Mr. Hauser and the priest. As they drove past the empty lot where the creamery once stood, Allie averted her eyes. The demise of the excellent local creamery at the hands of a corporation from up north still felt personal. Bandon's creamery had a fine reputation for putting out great cheeses, several varieties. They were the first to produce the delicious smoked cheese that she liked so much. The new company fired the workers and razed the building. Then they sold the Bandon label and recipes to a Wisconsin company. In protest, she never bought the northern company's cheese products.

41

Then they passed the big, white, stucco building that had housed Rita Ray's corner beauty shop. The shop was gone too, now, but the building evoked memories. Allie had her hair cut there many times when she was going to school in the late 50s and early 60s. She remembered Rita, the hairdresser who always did such a good job on her hair.

"You remember Rita Ray, don't you Sis? Didn't she have something tragic happen? I can't remember the details, can you? Didn't her husband have a terrible accident?"

Alicia sighed. "Yeah, I felt so bad for her. It happened after you went off to college."

RITA RAY

Rita Ray ran her beauty shop in the building at the bottom of the hill on the north end of town. She was tall and slim and wore her hair in a different fashionable hairstyle every week. It changed color frequently, too. She kept herself clean and neat, and her seashore themed shop in order. She was pretty in a slightly bucktoothed way and had large expressive brown eyes. A fourth generation Bandonian, she knew everyone, who was married to whom, and from what family, who was cheating with whom, and what her cousin, who cooked at the "Sassy Sea Fare" restaurant nearby, would serve for dinner that night. She knew who was sick with what, and how the fishing was going. She could tell you all about the shenanigans that went on behind the scenes at City Hall.

Rita was married to Ed, a sturdy, good-looking, hardy logger. They had three kids, Joey, age twelve, Grace, ten and Robbie, four. She had the older children come into the shop after school and do their homework in the little room behind the business end of the shop. Young Robbie stayed with his maternal grandmother while Rita worked. When the children showed up, the conversations were toned down from the often risqué discussions that went on among the women. Or they whispered their comments. There was frequent laughter and giggling.

Rita had an associate beautician, plump, middle-aged Amy Carson, a (very bleached) blonde, who did hair and facials. Suzy Long, who came in three times a week to do manicures and pedicures, completed the staff. The shop was a beehive of beauty activity. The smell of hair spray filled the air, and sometimes the place reeked of the eye-watering ammonia scent of permanent wave solution. Many of the older ladies in town came there to have their hair done and "blued" every week.

Rita was happy with her little business, her energetic, lovable logger and her children. She felt blessed and let the ladies know it. A strong Baptist, she attended the First Southern Rite Holy Baptist Church of Christ. But she was no prude and occasionally surprised her clients by cracking a ribald joke in spite of her Bible studies. She also didn't let her religious tendencies stop her from being the channel for various rumors and gossip that passed through the shop like the perpetual coastal breeze.

One day she was trimming Lorna Dorne's hair and the topic of the goings-on of the high school teachers came up. It appeared that a couple of them were busily engaged in after school activities that had nothing to do with the students. Lorna's daughter, Claire, had brought home the rumor going through the school about a certain teacher's wife who had been seen at the "salmon races" (the popular make-out spot on the bluff overlooking the ocean) with another teacher's husband. Also, she recounted the rumor that the football coach had been caught drunk, peeing on the neighbor's lawn. On top of that, one of the teachers had been sent packing when someone on the school board found out that he wasn't married to his "wife."

And, Lorna whispered, "One of the girls, who shall remain nameless, is pregnant by one of the football players and has to leave school. She's actually showing already."

Rita paused in mid-comb out. "Well, with the bad examples of the teachers, what do you expect?" She fluffed the curls around Lorna's face. "There, isn't that pretty? The school board needs to do something about that coach. But you know, as long as he's winning games they'll never fire him." She gestured with her comb, looking Lorna in the face in the mirror. "And those kids are getting out of control They listen to that awful Elvis and get all heated up and the next thing you know they're copying the adults. This new rock music is ruining our youth. My pastor said so just this Sunday. He's talking about havin' a record bonfire event."

Lorna, plump, middle-aged, with large baby-blue eyes, frowned and shifted in her seat, setting off her curls in a wave of protest. "That's a good idea. I can't believe some of the things that are happenin'. People are losing their morals."

Chubby, gray-haired Alvira, sitting in the second chair, spoke up. "There does seem to be some kind of a bad influence goin' on in this town. I'm glad I don't have to worry about my Jack picking up with some floozy. He's true blue to the core."

Rita chuckled to herself. Alvira's husband, fifty-ish, bald and fat, generally looked like an unmade bed. She couldn't picture any of the local "floozies" being interested in him.

Rita couldn't resist a bit of bragging. "I feel the same way about my Ed. He never looks at another woman twice. And I've seen them looking at him with evil intent, you know? I have complete faith in him." Rita adored her Ed more than she could say, and he reciprocated the feelings with boisterous enthusiasm. Being a logger, he maintained a tough, manly persona, but he was a marshmallow underneath. He frequently surprised Rita with a fistful of flowers, gleaned from the hillsides where he worked. He kept up the house and yard and adored his kids and spent many of his off-work hours with them. He rarely said, "I love you" in words, but Rita knew that she and the children were the center of his life.

Lorna reared back. "Don't you worry about him workin' in the woods? I saw in the paper last week that another young man was killed in the woods, down out of Port Orford. A tree landed on him. It's awful. He left a wife and four little children. It seems like someone gets killed just about every week."

Rita felt a twinge of anxiety surge through her body, then dismissed it from her mind. "I do worry, sometimes. But I put my faith in the Lord to look out for him. I say a prayer every time he goes out that door."

A couple of weeks later, the shop was quiet as Amy worked on her customer in her station, and Rita was putting rollers in Edna Perly's frizzy hair, when the little bell tinkled as her shop door opened. Bart Johnson, one of her husband's co-workers and friend, stood there. He was a big man, heavy set and jowly in middle age. His cheeks were bright red from constant exposure to the elements. He was wearing dirty, cut-off logger's pants and still had on his dusty cork boots.

There were tears in his eyes and his mouth and head hung in an expression of misery. His wife, Anne, stood by his side, her face somber. She had been crying. Rita's heart lurched and her hands froze where they were, clutching a curler. This had to be very bad.

"Rita, I need to have a word with you?" said Bart, in a subdued, gruff voice. All activity stopped, as Amy and her customer turned to look at the tense tableau.

"What's happened?" Rita quavered.

Bart sucked in a sharp breath and stepped closer to Rita, placing a clumsy hand on her shoulder. "I'm so sorry, Rita," he choked. "I have to tell you there's been an accident. Ed was driving the cat across that bridge goin' over that creek where we're workin' and the bridge collapsed." His eyes filled with tears. "He didn't make it. I am so sorry Rita, but he's gone."

Stunned silence. Then, "Oh my God!" Amy gasped.

Rita sat down abruptly. Her voice fluctuated. "He's dead? My Ed is gone?"

"I am so sorry..." Bart shifted awkwardly on his feet, twisting his hat in an agonized grip.

Anne rushed forward and put her arms around Rita. "Oh, Rita. I just don't know what to say. I'm so sorry."

Edna Perly made sympathetic noises, tears streaming down her face. She grabbed some tissues from a nearby box, twirled her chair around, squeezed out of it and handed several to Rita, using one herself. She put her hand on Rita's shoulder.

"Where is he?" Rita croaked. She felt like her heart had stopped. The whole world had stopped. Her life was over. She stared at the curler she still clutched in her hand. "I want to see him."

"They're takin' his body to the mortuary now. Is there anything we can do? Can we drive you there?"

Stunned, she looked blankly at Anne. "I want to see him." She stood up, dropped the curler on the counter. She glanced around. "Where are...what about the children?"

Edna began pulling curlers from her hair. "Don't you worry about the kids. I'll wait here until they get here. You go with Ann and Bart and do what you need to. I'll take'em over to your mom's."

Slowly, in a daze, Rita got her coat and purse. "Amy," she croaked, "would you lock the door and put up the closed sign when you leave?"

"Of course, Honey. You just go with them and do whatever needs to be done. I'll take care of everything." She sniffled. "I'm so sorry Rita. I just can't believe it."

"Thank you," Rita whispered. She went with Bart and Anne to face the end of her life as she knew it.

There was a huge turnout for the funeral. Most of the people in town knew and liked Rita and Ed. Both of their families were there to lend her their support. They all grieved the gentle son, husband, father who was now gone from their lives. The children were somber, lost, clinging to their mother and grandparents. Somehow, Rita made it through the funeral, cocooned in a wall of grief. The hymns, the eulogy were a buzz of sound in her brain. It went by in an agonizing blur.

At the potluck following the burial, her children clustered around her. She made short responses to the proffered sympathetic platitudes, not even registering who made them. But when some well-meaning person said, "Well, at least it was quick." Or "It's God's will," she wanted to hit them. If it was God's will she didn't want to have any more to do with Him. She kept the children close and tried to eat some of the generous potluck supper afterwards, but the food wouldn't go past the lump in her throat.

She stayed home for the next four weeks. Amy and Suzy kept the shop going and called her frequently. She thanked them but did not return to the shop. She kept the children out of school the first week. Her mother stayed with her for several days. After the children went back to school, Rita would close the door behind them and just spend the day caring for Robbie, not bothering to get dressed.

She couldn't see how she could spend the rest of her life without Ed. They had married as soon as she graduated from beauty school. They had "gone steady" for three years before that. Her whole life had revolved around him. What did she have to look forward to? A lonely old age. When Robbie went down for his afternoon nap, she crawled back into bed. She sleepwalked through the motions of everyday life for the sake of the children. When she allowed herself to feel anything, she was angry that the rest of the world went on about its normal business when her life was destroyed.

The children mourned in their own way and were very subdued. Allison and Robbie clung to her whenever possible. But they knew she was not really there. She would put her arms around them and hold them while staring into space. Or not hear if they asked questions. They had to physically tug on her to get her attention.

Ed's father had told Joey, "You're the man of the family now, Joey." Her son had taken that to heart and tried to fill in for his father wherever he could, mowing the lawn and doing chores. He didn't try to talk about his grief with his mother. Instead, he spent much of his time in his room, reading or doing his schoolwork. He stopped going out to play with his friends after school.

Ten-year-old Grace, too, tried to be helpful around the house, entertaining Robbie and sweeping the floor. She set the table for their meals. Sometimes she retreated to her room and played with her dolls. Her mother didn't seem to notice.

The children did their homework without being reminded. At night, when they were in bed, they cried for their dad. Robbie cried and asked for him often, unable to understand why this hole was suddenly in his life. Sometimes he would have tantrums for no good reason.

This went on for four more weeks. Friends, family, and pastor called or stopped by, often bringing casseroles, but Rita wasn't interested in talking to anyone. Her mother and father dropped in several times a week, as did Ed's parents, the only ones allowed in the house. They would try to console Rita, do maintenance chores, clean up the house a bit, and play with the children. Sometimes her mother, Gloria, stayed to cook dinner for the family. But Rita would just shuffle around in her slippers and robe, or her jeans and sweatshirt, unable to make more than monosyllabic replies to her mother's remarks.

Gloria scolded gently. "Rita, Honey, you just have to pull yourself together. The children need you. You're young. You have to make a life for yourself. Ed wouldn't want you to go on grieving like this. He would want you to make the most of your life."

Rita looked at her dully. "I just don't know how to do it, Mama. Without Ed, I just don't know how to live."

One afternoon, near the end of the month, she wandered into the kitchen. Idly, she opened the cupboard door and there was Ed's favorite coffee mug, right in front. He would never use it again. She stared at it and was hit by a spasm of rage. She grabbed it and threw it furiously across the room, where it made a satisfying crash against the counter, scattering pieces all over the place. How dare he be so selfish? Trying to drive a twenty-ton bulldozer across that rickety bridge? He was just showing off, the bastard. Overwhelmed by grief she leaned against the counter, sobbing and moaning. Was she going to feel this way the rest of her life?

Gradually, her sobs faded as she focused on the butcher knife on the counter. She reached for it, mesmerized by the thought of stopping the pain. She found herself standing at the kitchen sink with the sharp blade of the knife resting on the skin of her wrist. It would be so easy to just slice down and let the life drain away.

She felt an urgent tug on her robe and a worried little voice said, "Mommy?"

She gasped and dropped the knife with a clatter in the sink. Ed would be so ashamed of her.

She picked Robbie up and held him tightly and wept quietly while she nestled his head on her shoulder. There was nothing for it but to go on. She sat in the rocker and rocked Robbie for a long time. She thought about the day, four years earlier, when Robbie was born. Ed stood by her side, glowing at the sight of his new son, a big smile on his deeply tanned face. He stroked her cheek and kissed her gently on the lips. "He's a winner, Sweetheart. Thank you." Remembering his look of love made her heart turn. She tightened her grip on her baby, whispered, "I'll always be here for you, Robbie."

Eventually, she put Robbie down for his nap and then cleaned up the mess from the shattered mug. Then she stepped into the shower and scrubbed from head to foot, letting the soothing hot water wash over her body. She did her hair and carefully applied makeup. She held the makeup mirror close to her face, hardly recognizing herself. She saw new lines radiating out from the corners of her eyes and mouth. This was her "after" face, the one Ed would never see. She got dressed. Then she straightened up the house. When Robbie woke up, she took him to her mother's house and then went to the beauty shop, to let them know that she was coming back.

The following Monday, she was back at work, following her usual routine.

As she brought her mind back to the present, Allie glanced at Sophie. "I really felt sorry for Rita when her husband died. But she kept the shop going until she retired, didn't she?"

"Yeah. She always did a good job on my hair. A couple of years after her husband died, she remarried that insurance salesman, Jack Allen. Remember him? They did a lot of traveling after she finally retired. But they're both gone now."

"I'm glad she had a good life. She was young yet when Ed died."

They proceeded into the cemetery driveway.

I missed you more than ever then.

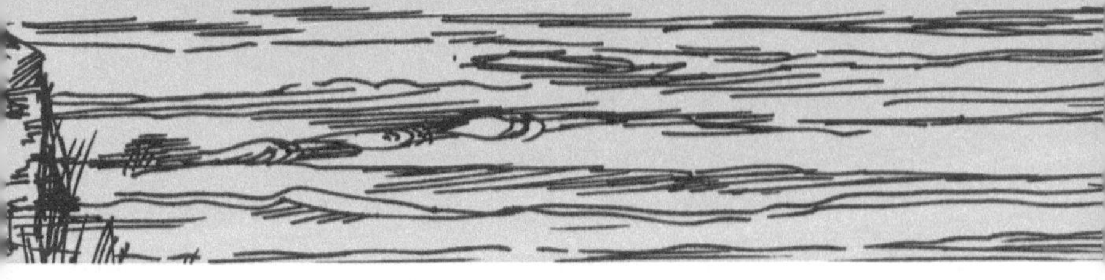

CHAPTER SEVEN

A SAILOR
AND HIS GIRL

ALLIE CAREFULLY CARRIED her mother's ashes to the gravesite, where the mortician quickly dug a deep hole just big enough for the urn. He then lowered it into the hole, and the priest said a blessing over it, while the girls joined in as he said the Lord's prayer. The priest made the Sign of the Cross, and chatted with the girls while the hole was filled. Then they all shook hands, and the two men left.

Allie and Sophie stayed on for a while, meditating over their parent's graves. Allie took some tissues from her pocket and blew her nose. Finally, she sighed, and took Sophie's hand. "They're together now, and it's fitting. Mom was just waiting for the end so she could join Dad."

Sophie sniffed. "You're right. These last few years were hard for her. I'm glad they're at peace together. I just wish the sibs could be here."

"Me too. But at least they made it to her church service at home." Allie looked up over the scene. "This graveyard holds so many memories and old friends and family. Grandma and Grandpa, our aunts and uncles, and Caleb and Lilly. Mom and Dad worked so hard to raise us all." She sniffed, wiped her nose, "And I love the view from up here. Let's look around a bit."

They wandered around, noting the names and dates of old friends and acquaintances. Lost in their own private thoughts, they drifted over near the edge of the bluff to look out at the harbor. The gray river flowed out to the blue-green sea through the north and south jetties. It looked calm and gentle from the edge of the hillside. A fogbank was moving in on the horizon, but overhead the sky was blue. The light breeze carried the mournful call of the foghorn as it sent its warning message to sea. The sound was always soothing to Allie when she was sad, and she loved this view. They watched as a fishing boat worked its way over the bar and up the river, finally nosing into the dock.

They started back towards their car when Allie paused by the grave of Norbert "Bert" Jensen. Next to him, resting under the double headstone, was his wife, Ruby.

"Sophie, remember those two? They were such an interesting and fun couple. Ruby was the object of a lot of gossip. Remember?"

"Oh, yeah. Mom used to know Ruby. She liked her, even if she was rough around the edges. But they weren't buddies."

NORBERT AND RUBY

Norbert was the mayor of the town for ten years. He was short, about five-feet-four. His wife, Ruby, was a head taller and ten years younger than he. Together they owned a pub, The Schooner, down on the main drag in old town. It was a favorite haunt of fishermen and loggers in the area.

Bert ran the town council with a relaxed attitude. He didn't sweat the small stuff. He did not have a "Napoleon complex." He basically left all the major decisions up to the consensus of the councilmen. There weren't any councilwomen in those days. But the councilmen pretty much took their wives' opinions into account when it came to running the town.

Well liked in the community, Bert belonged to the Lions and the Elks and the Chamber of Commerce. He fished and hunted with his friends and kept the pub well stocked with beer and ale and peanuts. The pub had a simple menu of sandwiches, chowder and hamburgers, and, of course, French-fries. The jukebox blared country music from 11 A.M., when they opened, until they closed at 1 A.M. Two pool tables in the back were quite popular.

Norbert's wife was a character. She was a wild woman and Bert was crazy about her. Bert met Ruby when he was in the Navy, stationed in San Diego. He and some of his pals went out one night for some R and R and headed for a pub in the seedier part of town. As they approached the building, he noticed, standing by the curb, a young, heavily made-up blonde girl wearing a tight, short skirt and a fake fur cape. She was obviously trying to catch the eye of one of the johns who cruised up and down the street. Something about her nervous, defensive manner, her haughty stance, caught Bert's heart as they approached. His friends started whistling and making nasty remarks as they came nearer. She turned, shot them a dirty look, and started walking away from them. She was apparently after bigger game.

Bert yelled at the men to shut up and leave her alone. One of his buddies started after her anyway, and Bert grabbed him and spun him around. The man stood a head taller than Bert, but that didn't give him a second's pause. "Leave the girl alone," he growled.

The man laughed and started to turn back. Bert grabbed his arm and repeated his warning. He jerked his arm away, but Bert persisted. "Leave that girl alone. I mean it, Ted."

Again, the man turned and headed after the girl and Bert got in his face. "I'm telling you. Leave her alone, or I'll punch your lights out, Ted. I'm serious."

Surprised, Ted snapped, "What's she to you? Go find your own bitch. I'm goin' after this one."

Bert may have been small, but he was powerful. He was the light-weight boxing champ of the whole Navy yard. He punched Ted in the gut so hard that he knocked the breath out of him. As the man stood there, bent double, gagging, gasping and clutching his stomach, Bert took off after the girl.

When he caught up with her, she quickened her pace, trying to get away. He ran after her. "Lady, lady, wait up. I just want to talk to you; I don't want to hurt you."

She slowed down and eyed him warily. "What do you want? You want a 'date'?"

"Please stop. I just want to talk." He looked at her. "How old are you?"

She eyed him sullenly. "Eighteen," she lied. "What's it to you?"

He smiled. "Just curious. Look, can we just get a cup of coffee somewhere? I'd really like to have someone to talk to."

"Well, I got to make some money. I can't just be talkin' to people for nothin.'"

"I'll pay you whatever the going rate is for an hour of your time." He grinned happily at her and somehow Ruby knew that she could trust this guy. She went with him for coffee in a shabby diner nearby.

Bert checked out her thin face. "You hungry?"

She eyed him, still wary. "I could eat."

"What's good here?"

"I dunno. Um, maybe the hamburgers? And fries?"

Bert ordered two 'burgers and fries and coffees.

They ate and talked late into the night. He found out that she had run away from her miserable home to escape a nagging mother and druggy stepfather who was always after her for sex. She met a man at the bus station, Jack Brood, who treated her kindly and said she could stay with him. It was an old story. He gave her pills, raped her, and began pimping her out on the streets. If she didn't bring in money, he beat her. She was terrified of him and desperate to find a way out.

Bert grew angrier by the moment as she told her story. Finally, he looked intensely into her eyes and said, "Ruby, you can't go back there. I'll take care of you. I'll find you a place to stay."

She stared at him and thought for a long time. At last, she said, "How do I know I can trust you? What do you want from me? Why would you do that? You don't even know me. And what if Jack finds me? I'm scared of him. He might kill me."

Solemnly, he held up his hand, boy scout style, and swore, "I would never let that happen. I'll find you a safe place. I'll look after you. I won't ask anything from you except that you stay clean and maybe finish your high school education. And when you're really eighteen, I'm gonna marry you if you'll have me. What do you say?"

She reared back, frowning. "I say you're crazy. What makes you think I'd want to marry you?"

He gave her his engaging grin. "Maybe you don't want to now, but you will. I'm gonna woo you, Ruby. If you don't want to marry me by the time I'm discharged, I'll not bother you anymore. Deal?" He held out his hand. Her face settled into a solemn expression; she took it.

Ruby went with him right then and there. He put her up at a hotel for the night and booked a room for himself. He escorted her to her room, handed her the key, and told her to lock the door and not open it for anyone but him in the morning.

The next morning, he knocked on the door. She opened it hesitantly, peeked out and smiled at him for the first time. She gathered her bag, into which she had stuffed the complimentary soaps and shampoos, and they went out for breakfast.

He had a surprise for her. "Ruby, I have an aunt living here in the Sun Ray suburb. She's raised her kids and living all alone now. I called her last night and asked her if she'd take you in for a while, until I get out of the navy, and we can get married. She was real excited to have you. She's been lonely and craving company. If you want, you can go back to school in the area and get your high school diploma. She said she'd sign up for you. Would you like that?"

Ruby teared up. "Why'd she do that for me? She don't even know me."

"I'll pay your room and board. It'll help her out with her finances. And she loves young people. She's always been my favorite aunt. Aunt Myrtle. She'll love you."

And so, it came about that Ruby went to live with Bert's aunt until she graduated from high school two years later and Bert was discharged.

Bert and Ruby had corresponded for two years, whenever he was at sea, getting to know each other better and better. Ruby realized that she loved her little sailor. No one had ever been so kind or so loyal to her. She felt that he was her destiny.

Myrtle and Ruby both cried when Bert came to take his girl home. Ruby looked very grown up when he arrived. She was dressed in a snug sweater and jeans, and still wore glamorous makeup. She was still the Ruby he first saw. But she had lost some of the rough edges, thanks to Myrtle's care, and the defiance was gone from her eyes. The women hugged each other, and both promised to write.

Bert took Ruby back home to Bandon, where they were married at the local Episcopalian church, with Bert's parents and brother and sister in attendance.

They rented a cozy little house in a pleasant neighborhood above old town, and Bert invested his savings in the pub. They had a big grand opening, and half the town showed up. The place took off and was steadily busy from then on.

Ruby was frequently the subject of town gossip. She bleached her hair a bright, yellow blonde, wore too much makeup, and gaudy, sparkly jewelry. She loved to dress up in bright clothing that showed off her figure, which was luscious and an object of envy on the part of the female populace. She frequently used language that would make a logger blush. She rode a Harley around the back roads of the county. She was known to hold the unofficial speed record between Bandon and Coquille. This was some feat, as the two-lane highway was narrow and winding and followed the river most of the way. Teenage boys vied with each other to see who could make the trip the fastest, but they never beat Ruby's time.

And she didn't stay home and cook and clean house like a good housewife was supposed to do. She worked at the pub alongside of Bert.

Bert took a lot of teasing on Ruby's account from the loggers, fishermen and millworkers who frequented his establishment. But Bert just gave it back in kind, as did Ruby. He was never jealous of the men who came in and mooned over her, because she knew how to handle the testosterone-laden and could put a drunk on the floor with a twist of her wrist. She doted on her little husband and he knew it. Nobody tried to manhandle Ruby because they all knew just how low was her tolerance level. She had an acid tongue that could cut like a fish knife. And the locals all liked her and wouldn't stand for any monkey business where she was concerned. God help the tourist who tried to fondle her. They considered her to be one of their own and took offense on her behalf. And besides, Bert kept a baseball bat behind the counter, which he was known to use to good effect. All in all, things went smoothly at the pub.

Bert and Ruby had a son. They called him Sammy, and he was the light of their lives. Sammy was short, like his father, about five feet five inches when he was fully grown. He was a brain and got straight A's. He took his share of abuse from the bigger boys.

Bert decided that Sammy needed to learn to box. He bought some gloves, put up a punching bag in the garage, and proceeded to teach the boy how to defend himself.

Sammy was twelve when the lessons started, and determined to impress his father, whom he adored. He worked hard at it, and as he grew, developed powerful muscles and fighting techniques. The bullies learned not to mess with him. And they learned very quickly never to make nasty remarks about his glamorous mother, either.

But Bert and Ruby made sure their boy knew when to take a stand and when to walk away. They didn't want him to get into trouble at school or to become a bully himself.

Sam heeded their words. Besides, he was a mellow soul and empathized with underdogs of all kinds. He was known for his good nature and ability to tease and be teased. Because of this, Sam was very popular and well-liked by his classmates.

In high school, Sammy went out for the football team. Football, basketball, baseball and track were the only sports available at the school in those days. Sam was regularly pummeled as the team practiced for the upcoming season. He gamely kept at it, though. He was small but he was fast so he went out for the position of quarterback. The coach liked him but kept him on the second string because Bobbie Brown was bigger and faster, so he was first string quarterback. Plus, his dad was very influential on the School Board, and the coach wanted to keep on his good side. Besides, the coach insisted on winning games, so Sammy sat on the bench a lot.

Ruby and Norbert were apprehensive about their small son playing with the big brutes but didn't want to hold him back. They never missed a game, in spite of their business.

One night, in the middle of a tough game with the team from Coquille, Bandon High School's archrival, the coach was forced to put Sammy in because his star quarterback was injured. The game was tied so Coach Connor wasn't happy. But Sam was thrilled.

He had barely entered the game, and had caught the ball, when the lights suddenly went out. For five minutes, everything was black and confusion reigned. People sat, noisily yelling for lights and cracking jokes, wondering what was happening as the stadium crew worked to solve the problem. The lights finally came back on to reveal Sam, sitting under the goalpost, holding the ball and beaming broadly.

The crowd looked on in amazement, then pandemonium broke loose. They roared and cheered and laughed. But the referee refused to count it as a goal. The Bandon crowd booed and screamed and threw things onto the field. The referee threatened to forfeit the game if they didn't calm down, so, gradually, peace was restored.

Ruby was incensed. Who did that referee think he was? Bert, who just laughed about the whole thing, had to hold Ruby back from storming the field. Their boy had made a touchdown and that was all there was to it. In the dark, yet! He finally got her calmed down as the game resumed.

The team from Coquille hadn't laughed at Sammy's little joke. In fact, they were steamed. So, as the final quarter progressed in the rain and mud, they were gunning for Sammy. In the last ten seconds of the game, with only six yards to go, Sammy managed to break through their defense and score the winning touchdown. But he ended up under a pile of Coquille players. When they finally clambered off from him, he lay still on the ground. The wild cheering stopped as the crowd realized that Sammy was seriously hurt.

The coaches and referees ran to Sammy as his teammates gathered around. The Bandon crowd, which ordinarily would have been erupting in jubilation at this point, was silent and holding its collective breath. Ruby and Bert ran down the stadium steps and out onto the field as a stretcher was brought up.

The coaches examining Sammy carefully turned him over. His face was a bloody mess, and his nose had been smashed flat. He opened his eyes and stared blearily at the faces looking down on him. "Did we win?" he wanted to know.

"We sure did," grinned coach Connor, relief in his voice.

Sammy smiled and closed his eyes as they carried him off the field with his parents walking on each side of the stretcher.

The band started playing the school song at a frantic pace and the stands erupted in wild cheers. But the Bandon players ignored that as they waded into the Coquille boys and began a fight that turned into a legendary riot on the field before the combined coaches, city and state police and school authorities could get it under control.

Meanwhile, as there was no ambulance service at that time, Sam's parents rushed him to Coos Bay, normally a forty-five minute drive, breaking every speed limit on the way. He was bleeding profusely and in serious pain as a frantic Ruby held his head against her shoulder and pressed a towel filled with ice against his poor nose. They got the bleeding stopped at the Coos Bay hospital, gave him drugs for the pain, then sent him on to Eugene, another two hours of driving, to have surgery done in the hospital there.

When it was all over, Sammy was left with a nose that looked like a prizefighter's. The kids at school thought it was cool and for a while Sam was the hero of the town.

But Sam had decided that he was never playing football again. His parents were secretly relieved and fully supported him in that decision.

So, in the spring he went out for the baseball team and, eventually, won a reputation as the finest pitcher in the league. He was student body president his senior year, lettered in baseball, and managed to keep a straight four-point GPA. His parents beamed with pride when he graduated at the head of his class and gave the commencement speech.

Sam went on the graduate from Willamette University and became a well-known lawyer in the state capitol. He never moved back to Bandon, but he saw his parents frequently. He married a lovely co-ed named Susanna, in a classy ceremony at the Episcopal Church in Salem.

Ruby made a big splash at the wedding in a broad-brimmed black hat and a tight fitting sexy red dress. Susannah's mother, wearing a tasteful peach colored outfit, looked at Ruby and choked. Somehow, she regained her composure and greeted Ruby and Bert with a cool, sugary smile before they were all seated for the ceremony. Ruby was unconcerned about the disapproving glances. Her darling son was madly in love and marrying a beautiful, classy girl. She was happy.

Eventually, Sammy and Suzanna had three children, two boys and a girl. Suzanna did her best to limit Ruby's influence on the children, which meant that they seldom came to Bandon to visit their grandparents.

Ruby and Bert adored their grandkids. Ruby even curbed her language around them. She knew that Susanna did not approve of her and bent over backwards whenever her daughter-in-law was around to please her and win her over. Eventually, Susanna learned to appreciate the love that Ruby had to offer. But she never quite trusted Ruby with the children, and rarely left her alone with them. However, the children loved Ruby and Bert. They were so much more fun than their stuffy, uptight WASP grandparents.

Ruby and Bert finally sold their business and retired. Ruby talked Bert into buying matching Harley's with matching trailers and they took off and rode across the country. They toured the east coast and were coming back through the south when Bert was run down by a doped-up trucker near Phoenix. Ruby was fighting shock as she rode the ambulance back to the hospital. Once there, she succumbed to hysteria and had to be sedated. Bert died in surgery forty minutes later.

The staff was kind to Ruby, helping her place a call to Sam, comforting her and helping her arrange for Bert's transportation back to Oregon.

Sam joined Ruby in Phoenix and they flew to Portland together. His family met them there and they followed the hearse back to Bandon. Together, they buried their beloved Norbert in the cemetery on the hill, overlooking the harbor.

Sam and his family stayed for several days, but finally had to get back to their life in Salem. Over the years, they tried to talk Ruby into moving up near them, but she always refused. Bandon was her home and besides, she couldn't leave Bert. She lived in her little house for the rest of her life. She visited Bert frequently on the hill, gazing out to sea and listening to the foghorn as the evening mist rolled in.

"Darlin', the auxiliary had a dinner last Friday. You'd of loved it. We had dancin' and a great potluck. I missed you more than ever then. There's no joy in doin' stuff alone. So, I carried you in my heart and danced with some of the guys and pretended they were you." She would tell him about what she would have for dinner that night, and what was happening on their favorite TV shows.

She kept busy with the Lion's Club auxiliary, and with going's on at the church. She had never been a regular churchgoer but became one after she was widowed. It gave her connection with her community and she even became friends with some of the ladies. Occasionally she would drop by the pub, just to see how the new owner was treating it and drink a beer in Bert's honor. She noted the changes to relate to Bert. She spent the holidays in Salem with Sam and his family.

But she never looked at another man. And she never rode a Harley again.

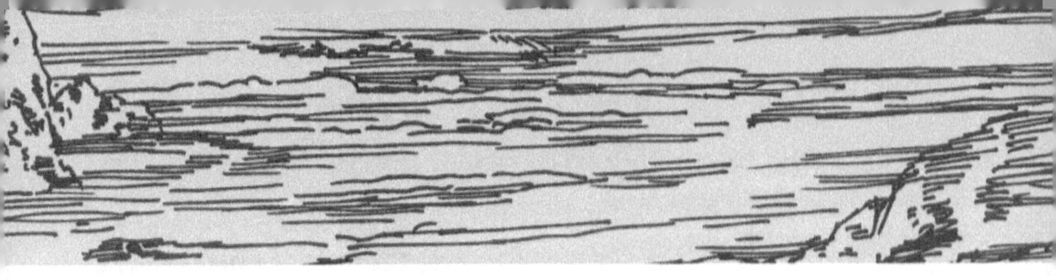

CHAPTER EIGHT

GIRLS' REBELLION

ALLIE AND SOPHIE left the cemetery and drove through the town. Allie aimed the car up the hill to the south and, turning right, passed the grade school, then the high school, the scene of their teenage angst and torment,

"Gosh, remember what four years in this school was like? I never fit in with most of the class. The kids were either the popular ones, or the disinterested wild ones. Some of them were so mean. I only had a few friends. Don't know how I'd of survived without 'em. I couldn't wait to graduate."

Sophie narrowed her eyes at the building. "God, yeah. I hated it here. Was so glad to get out."

Allie sighed. "You had a bunch of mean girls in your class."

"You know it!" Sophie replied.

"They were jealous of you because you were so pretty. I'm sorry you had to endure that. But, really, the girls all had it rough. If you didn't have a 'steady' boyfriend, you were nothing."

"True. I never dated any of the lame boys in my class. In fact, I didn't date until I was in college."

67

"Dating was dangerous. I can't help rememberin' Melody Newcastle. She was just a year ahead of me. I've often thought about her."

Sophie looked at Allie. "She was four years ahead of me but I was vaguely aware of her. I just realized that she was gone one day." They drove on in silence.

MELODY NEWCASTLE

Allie was lost in remembering. Melody was the golden girl. The most popular in school. She had that glossy, brunette flip that brushed her shoulders and never lost its curl. Tall and willowy, she wore the straight, slim skirts and sweaters of the day with style. Melody made a point of talking to girls who were less popular and were charmed by her attention. Her teachers all enjoyed her polite and intelligent demeanor. She was a cheerleader, an honor student, active in several clubs and activities. Allie wondered how she also found the time to excel at basketball, softball, and track. Only the most popular girls hung out with her. But everyone liked her.

"Melody was way above my league," said Allie. "The boys all wanted her, the girls all wanted to be her. But she had a 'steady.' So, the other boys had to be content with lustful watching, and the girls were placated because she was out of action."

"Oh yeah, I remember Melody. Didn't she date Dan Jackson? They went together for a couple of years, I think. Then they broke up."

Allie grimaced. "Her senior year. I idolized her. After the breakup, I started feeling sorry for her. I saw her arguing with Dan one day at lunchtime. Pretty soon, they weren't going together anymore. I noticed she wasn't wearing his class ring either. She started acting differently, reserved and serious, and didn't go out for girls' basketball that winter. She started to look a bit plump. The rumors whizzed around her. Girls were speculating in the locker room."

"Did you notice Melody's putting on weight?"

"Why'd they break up? Is Dan going with someone else?"

"D'you think she's preggers?" Gradually, the girls all became aware that, yes, she was pregnant. This was catastrophic in 1957. We all knew she'd have to leave school once she started showing. It made Allie angry. Why should Melody take all the blame? Why did girls always have to pay the price?

A pregnant girl had two options. If the boy was manly enough, he "did the right thing" and married her. If not, the girl would have to leave school, maybe leave town to stay with distant relatives, give the baby up for adoption before returning with some kind of cover story. She would then either go back to school or get a job. Or sometimes, stay away and finish her education wherever she had gone.

It became apparent that Melody wasn't getting married. The boys whispered among themselves about her, and Dan spread the rumor that she was easy. One of Allie's guy friends told her about it. She was livid and told him that was a lie. But it didn't make any difference in the atmosphere in school.

Melody bravely kept coming to school. She wanted her education. A top-notch student, she could be seen studying between classes or at lunch hour, her face in her books. She looked so sad to Allie. It was only a matter of time, as her belly began to show more, before she would be asked to drop out of school. The girls in her circle pretended not to notice but tried to avoid her. She was tainted goods. Allie was angry that Dan hadn't stepped up to the plate. It was all so unfair. She began to talk to her friends about how they should stick up for Melody. Word began to spread among the girls. Many of them were angry at the double standards of the day.

One fine day, at lunchtime, Melody took her lunch out on the front lawn of the school and sat on the grass in the sun. She looked very lonely there, eating by herself. Allie decided she had to do something. She strolled out on the lawn and sat beside Melody. She reached into her bag and offered Melody an apple. Melody shook her head but thanked her. A faint smile curved her lips. "Aren't you afraid of being contaminated?"

Allie smiled back. "As far as I know it isn't catching. And it makes me mad the way everyone acts around you. I still like you and don't care who knows it."

Melody's eyes glistened. "Thanks, Allie."

They ate together in companionable silence. Slowly, more of the girls wandered out and sat down around her. Soon, they were all laughing and chatting. Before long, more girls had seen what was happening and joined the rest, quietly, defiantly. The girls were showing the rest of the school that they were on Melody's side. They spent the whole noon hour there, most of the senior and junior girls surrounding her, jabbering as girls will do. They tossed food items back and forth, sharing and talking about anything and everything. "Are you going to the game Friday night?" "Did you see that cute new boy in biology?" "Where'd you get your hair cut? It looks great." And so on. One of the girls pulled out a bottle of nail polish and started doing Melody's nails. Allie felt like it was an open rebellion against the norms of their society. The girls always had to suffer the shame and punishment. The guys just got off scot-free. It had to change.

Melody stayed in school for two more weeks and the rest of the girls continued to stick by her, even some of the cheering squad. They would meet her at her locker and go to class with her, hang out with her at lunchtime. Mr. Johnson, the principal, frowned when he saw them walk by, clustered around her. But one day he called Melody into the office. Her mother was there. After that Melody disappeared from school.

Allie wondered where she'd gone, but none of her friends knew either. Or at least, if they knew, they weren't saying.

The girls muttered among themselves about Dan, and how none of them would ever date him again. Dan got along fine with the boys, but many of the girls shut him out. In desperation, he even asked Allie out. She was standing alone at her locker when she felt this presence looming over her. Startled, she jumped back. She stared at him, as he glanced furtively around the hall. He was tall, with dark curly hair and chiseled features. Ordinarily, she would have been flattered. But she knew that the other girls had turned him down. And she intensely disliked him for what he'd done to Melody. Normally, he wouldn't have given her the time of day.

He casually leaned against the front of the locker next to her and asked her to go to the movies with him that Saturday. He glanced around to see if anyone was watching.

"After what you did to Melody, there's no way I'd ever go out with you."

His shocked expression was comical. He stepped back, his face turned red, and he glared at her. He couldn't believe she'd turned him down.

"Fine. You can go to hell." He whipped around and walked off stiffly. Allie resisted the urge to kick his backside.

After several months, Melody finally came home. She spent a week with her parents and then moved to her aunt's house in Eugene. She sent a note to Allie, thanking her for sticking up for her, and explained that she would finish her schooling in Eugene. Allie wrote back, but there was no reply.

Allie often wondered what happened to her, or her baby. She sighed. "I'm glad I never went steady with any of those boys. It was kind of painful not to be popular, but I was better off without it. Several of the girls in my class married right out of high school. I doubt that they've had a good life. I'm glad you and I waited until we were ready and found the right husbands."

Sophie nodded. "For sure. We were really lucky. What d'you suppose the guys are doin' without us there? I'll bet they're fishing together and enjoyin' the freedom. Probably getting their share of beer."

Allie laughed. "I'll bet they're havin' a great time. No doubt about that. I'm so glad they're friends."

They drove on down to the Beach Loop, the street that ran along the bluff, where all the nicest houses were, and where Melody once lived. Allie wondered wistfully if Melody was living in a nice home, like one of these, with a loving family. Or maybe she'd gone on to have a satisfying career? She hoped so.

CHAPTER NINE

THE UGLY DUCKLING

AS THEY SLOWLY DROVE along the familiar street, Allie again flashed back to the past. "I'm really rolling down Memory Lane, Soph. Gosh, remember Rose Fletcher?"

"Oh yeah. She was special, wasn't she?"

"She sure surprised me. She was a grade behind me, but everybody knew everybody back then, by sight if not by name. She wasn't like the girls who mooned over the junior and senior boys. The guys in our own age groups were so immature. Or so we thought. She didn't seem to notice or care."

Sophie sighed. "Gosh, Rose really bowled us over, didn't she?" She slapped her knee and laughed. "I loved it!"

ROSE FLETCHER

She seemed almost invisible, did Rose Fletcher. She was homely, with a big nose, swarthy, pock-marked skin, and horn-rimmed glasses. Her mousy brown hair hung limply in a loose pageboy style. She wore drab colors, no makeup, and loose-fitting garments. She reminded Allie of a little gray wren.

Smart, and a good student, Rose was quiet and reserved. The bullies didn't pick on her. She was just mostly ignored. She slipped down the hallways between classes with a fluidity and grace that few noticed, avoiding eye contact with others. Usually, she ate lunch with one of her plain friends. Who would have guessed that under her baggy sweaters and skirts there lurked a lovely, lithe feminine figure? But there came a time when she finally received the attention she deserved.

The big event every year, for most of the town, was the high school band concert. The school had a fine band and scattered among the students, were some very talented people. The annual concert was highly anticipated by all the parents and student body. It was a chance for some of the more musically talented youngsters to show what they could do. The Spring Concert in 1957 was no exception. Excited students, parents, and townspeople packed the gymnasium where the concert was staged.

The band opened with a rousing National Anthem, followed by a Sousa march, then a couple of Glen Miller pieces. Steve Frank, a fantastic pianist, played Joplin's "Maple Leaf Rag" and "The Entertainer." The crowd clapped loudly after each rendition. Then Mr. Brown, the beloved bandleader, announced that they would next be featuring a special act. Mrs. Logan, the local dance instructor, had recommended to him a very special student. "Please welcome the lovely ballet artistry of Miss Rose Fletcher."

The audience clapped politely.

Allie turned to Sophie and whispered, "What? Did you know she was a dancer?"

Sophie shook her head, wide-eyed. "Not a clue."

Lilting strains of "Swan Lake" began as a vision in a diaphanous, shimmering white gown flowed out onto the stage into the spotlight. Allie gasped, as did several people around her. Rose was beautiful. Her mousy hair was caught in a bun on top of her head, surrounded by a sparkling tiara. The thick glasses were gone. She wore makeup, with pale pink lipstick and blush giving her face a rosy glow. Her lithe figure floated and twirled, bent and swayed to the music as she leapt back and forth on the stage in a fantastic storm of grace. She glimmered and gleamed, her face glowed.

Allie sat, awestruck. Who knew Rose could transform herself like this? Entranced, her mouth dropped in surprise, she watched the lovely scene unfold. When the performance was done, and the swan had fluttered gracefully to the floor in the final movement, all was quiet for a moment. Then the audience erupted with loud cheering and clapping in a standing ovation. Rose curtsied gracefully as the crowd continued the roar of approval for several minutes. Her proud father walked up and gave her a bouquet of red roses. She blushed as she accepted them, beaming all the while, and waving to the audience. Finally, she exited the stage with her flowing dancer's stride. Allie was still amazed. How had she not noticed—had Rose moved through the halls like that?

The following Monday at school Rose was surrounded by well-wishers. She was smiling shyly and blushing at the same time. It was wonderful to see her blooming like that. Allie noticed that from then on, she walked with a more confident stride as she went through the halls. The other kids noticed her and greeted her as they walked by. She smiled more and spoke out more in class. As time went by, her clothes became more colorful and better fitting. She was still plain, but she was somebody.

Rose performed at all the Spring Concerts until she graduated. She received a scholarship to the University of Oregon. Allie didn't follow her career after that, but she tried harder never to take her marginalized classmates for granted. And she never forgot the beauty of Rose's moment of glory.

Allie pulled into the parking space at the south jetty. "Why don't we spend some time on the beach before we go to dinner? Who knows when we'll be back down here."

Sophie unfastened her seat belt. "You bet. I need a beach fix. Let's go."

They picked their way down to the sand and stayed until the sun went down.

CHAPTER TEN

THE TOWN DOG

THE NEXT DAY, following breakfast, Allie aimed the car on towards "The Bluff," as everyone called it. It was a high point of land overlooking the shore and had recently been developed into a park-like setting, with trails along the crest of the bluff. The trail down to the beach was steep, and in the 40s and 50s the kids mostly used the parking area to "watch the salmon races." Now there was a wooden stairway down to the sand. The girls gazed out over the monolithic basalt outcroppings that rose from the waves, watching the water dash against the sides, creating great plumes of spray shooting into the air.

Sophie broke the silence. "Remember Shadow? She was always at the beach, dragging sticks around so people could throw them into the waves for her to fetch? She was really a neat dog."

Allie smiled. "I couldn't forget Shadow. Loved that dog."

SHADOW

Shadow was everybody's beach dog. The coal-black lab appeared on the beach by the south jetty one day in the spring of 1962. Her shiny black coat was marked only by a light tan, spidery splotch on her chest. No one knew where she came from or who her owner was. There was no collar or nametag around her neck.

Gradually, she became the town dog. The local folk would look for her when they went to the beach. She lived to chase after sticks, preferably thrown out into the water. She would pick up a piece of driftwood and carry it to anyone who was wandering on the sands and drop it at their feet. Then she would look up expectantly, tail wagging, mouth grinning, waiting for the human to throw it out into the surf. If the person walked off, ignoring her, she would pick it up and run after him and drop it again in front of his feet. Eventually, the human would get the idea and throw it. In the event someone was just too dense to understand what was needed, or continued to ignore her, she would pick up her stick and find someone else. When the stick was thrown, she would bark joyfully and dash madly after it. Then she'd retrieve it and bring it back to be thrown again. She could keep it up for hours.

One day, Mary Sage and her husband were walking with some of their friends on the beach, when the lab approached with her stick. Mary threw the stick as far as she could into the surf. "We need to give her a name, don't you think?"

Her husband, Steve, thought for a minute. "Maybe we should call her 'Patch' because of the tan spot on her chest."

Other names were thrown out, "Blackie," "Water Dog," "Spider," and so forth. Finally, Mary said, "No, we should call her 'Shadow,' because of her black coat and her mysterious way of appearing and disappearing whenever she wants." They all liked it so "Shadow" she became to the townspeople. Eventually, she seemed to accept the name and would respond when people called her, bringing her inevitable stick.

No one knew where she went at night, but she would appear in the morning, after scavenging around town for whatever morsels she could find. A couple of the merchants would sometimes leave food outside their back doors for her. She would eat and then head for the beach.

Mavis Wentworth loved dogs. She had taken in a stray black and white mutt six years previously, and, when the stray produced two puppies, she kept those too. She never knew or cared about their lineage, but she did take the precaution of having them all neutered. They filled up her days with pampering them, and her heart with love, and helped fill the void left in her life when her beloved Hal died.

She took her pets, Jackie, Trudy and Axel to the beach whenever the weather permitted, to let them run. But Shadow melted her heart. She would let her dogs romp with Shadow and threw sticks into the waves for her. When Shadow came close, she would bend down and speak soothingly to her. Shadow allowed her to pat her sleek black head and listened expectantly to her babble. But she listened only so long and then would start barking until Mavis would throw her stick.

Mavis tried to coax Shadow into her car, so she could take her home, but the dog could not be coaxed. She brought bowls of food and water whenever she came to the beach. Shadow would happily devour every morsel, then slurp up the water. Soon, other people noticed Shadow hanging around where Mavis fed her in the parking area, and also began bringing doggy treats. She seemed to be thriving on the donated offerings.

Mavis put an ad in the Western World, and in the Coos Bay Times, trying to find her owner. No one called. She fretted. Poor Shadow! She had no one to care for her. Strays usually ended up dead, one way or another. There was no local animal shelter. Mavis talked to Big Al at the police station, but he told her that he had tried to capture Shadow, and she was just too elusive. He didn't have time to be running after every stray dog that wandered through town.

Mavis discussed the problem with her veterinarian. Harry Long was sympathetic, but non-committal. "What do you want me to do, Mavis? She seems to be doing pretty well on her own. Everybody looks out for her."

"Could you just at least come and look at her? Just to be sure she's healthy? I think we can get close enough to catch her. If I could just get her home, I think I could get her to stay with me. She's a sweet dog. She's friendly and approaches people to play with her."

Harry sighed. He loved animals too and had heard about Shadow. He hated to think she might end up getting hit by a car or sick from eating garbage. And plump, seventyish, Mavis was one of his favorite clients. Her three much— loved mutts were brought to him regularly for maintenance. He sighed. "Well, um, okay. I'll see what I can do. Can you meet me on the beach next Sunday at about ten o'clock? I'll try to get a look at her."

Mavis thanked him profusely as he gently backed her out of his office.

Sunday morning Mavis met the vet at the graveled parking area by the south jetty. Together they walked south on the beach, looking for Shadow.

Finally, they spotted her, trotting toward them with her stick. Mavis called her to them, setting out the food bowl. Shadow approached and, carefully setting down her stick, began eating. Harry squatted down beside her and looked her over.

"She's thin and her fur's a little patchy." He patted her and rubbed behind her ears. He felt along her ribs. Shadow backed away nervously. "She looks like she was somebody's pet and got away. There's a line around her neck where the hair's been rubbed off. Maybe she escaped from somebody traveling through."

Mavis smoothed the sleek head. "D'you think you could help me get her into my car? I'd love to take her home, even though I have enough critters already."

"If you're willing to take her on, I'll try to help you. She's pretty big and strong but the two of us might be able to handle her. If you bring her into my office on Monday, I'll give her a thorough once-over and give her whatever shots I think she might need. Check her for worms and ear mites too."

Mavis picked up the food dish and slowly walked up the beach towards her car. Shadow picked up her stick and followed along. As they neared the car, Mavis put the bowl down and poured some water into it. Shadow dipped her head and began lapping it up. After she'd had time to slake her thirst, Mavis knelt and started petting her, murmuring endearments. Mavis was the only one who had been able to get this close to Shadow. Harry reached down and gently scooped up the dog in his powerful arms. Shadow yelped and wriggled wildly, trying to get away.

"Open the door, Mavis, and we'll put her in."

Mavis opened the back door and Harry tossed the struggling dog inside and slammed it shut. Shadow began barking loudly.

"If you can get her settled in, I'll see you in my office on Monday. D'you think you can handle her when you get home?"

"I'd appreciate it if you could follow me and help me get her into the yard. I'm only about a half mile from here."

"Okay. Lead the way."

So it was that Shadow found a new home. She had a padded bed in the utility room next to the younger dogs, Trudy and Axel. The pups' mother, Jackie, slept on her own pad in Mavis' bedroom. Mavis would only tolerate one dog in her room at night. They always started the night in their own beds, but, frequently, Mavis would wake up with Jackie's warm body curled up against her.

Shadow seemed content to play in the yard with the other three. She filled out from the regular meals and her coat began to look smoother and glossier. Mavis was pleased that she fitted in so well. She enjoyed watching her menagerie playing around in the yard.

About three weeks later, Mavis glanced out into the yard as she was tidying up at the sink and couldn't see Shadow. The other three were lazing in the sun in the backyard. Mavis went out, looked around and realized that Shadow was gone. She checked along the fence line surrounding the yard and came upon a hole, freshly dug. So that's how Shadow escaped! She was surprised that the other three hadn't followed suit. They watched with interest as she grabbed a shovel out of the shed and filled in the hole, tamping it down firmly. She would have to figure out some way to prevent hole digging in the future.

She looked at her curious menagerie and smiled. "You are such good doggies for staying home. I'm so proud of you." She petted and praised them for a while, then straightened up. "Well, I'll bet I know where that bad dog went. We'll go and find her." She took the dogs down to the beach. Sure enough, there was Shadow, romping in the surf with her stick. Mavis sighed in exasperation. What now? She would have to lure Shadow back near the car and try to get her to go in herself. She let her menagerie romp on the beach for a while and then called them in to go home.

Apparently, Shadow decided she'd had enough running that afternoon, and followed the other dogs into the car with only a little coaxing. That night she settled right down on her cozy bed in the utility room.

Mavis let the dogs out the next day. Of course, Shadow dug herself out again and was gone. Mavis went through the same routine as the day before. Baffled, she called Harry, and he suggested that she might have a dog run put in. Mavis couldn't afford a dog run. She could barely afford to feed the dogs. Finally, she decided that she would just let Shadow out in the morning and let her go. She would see if she came back in the evening when she got hungry.

As she had hoped, Shadow came back that evening, hungry, cold and looking for a warm place to sleep. So that's the way things went for some time, with Shadow hanging out at the beach in the daytime and coming home in the evening.

On a beautiful, golden day in September, house-weary Golda Bronson looked out her kitchen window while doing the breakfast dishes. She put down her dishtowel and stared. The sun was out, there was just a whisper of a breeze blowing and she was tired of being cooped up in the house. She whirled around and grinned at four-year-old Bobbie. "We're going to the beach."

He danced around, waving his arms. "Yay. Beach." She tossed together a picnic lunch, gathered up the beach buckets and toys, pulled jackets on Bobbie, Sondra (age two) and Lilly (six months). She packed bottles of formula and diapers in the diaper bag, along with many snacks. Then she donned her own jacket and stashed the children in the car. Ten minutes later she was at the beach.

Spreading out a beach towel, she placed Lilly upon it, poked an umbrella handle into the sad to shade her, and handed Bernie and Sondra their beach toys. "Now you two be good and stay right here by Mommy." They settled down, digging in the sand, while Lilly lolled in her little carrier and played with her rattles and blew bubbles. Golda sat down in the warm sand with her back against a convenient log. Why hadn't she done this more often? It was heavenly. Before long, having not had an uninterrupted night's sleep in four years, she nodded off.

The children happily dug in the sand for a while. But soon they were looking for more adventure. The slow waves lapping up on the shore drew their attention and they wandered off to investigate.

Shadow watched them with interest. Her ears pricked up. Tail wagging, she followed them. They played with pretty rocks, poked sticks in the sand. Then, as they dipped their toes into the water, Shadow became restless. She knew these tiny humans should not be there. She knew the power of the waves. She began to pace nervously back and forth and, looking at their mother, let out a worried whine. Golda did not respond.

A wave pushed in and lapped over little feet. The children giggled and pulled back. Shadow began to bark and trotted towards them. A wave came in and forcefully covered the children's ankles. Bernie stepped back quickly but Sondra lost her footing, landing on her hands and knees with a shriek. Shadow streaked forward and got between them and the waves, trying to herd them towards the sand. Bernie managed to back away, but Sondra screamed and got a mouthful of water. Another wave washed over the screaming child and began to drag her out as it receded. Shadow again tried to shoulder her away from the water, barking frantically all the while, and when that didn't work, she grabbed the hood of the child's jacket in her teeth and began dragging her back to the sand.

By now, Golda was wide awake and running for the children, as were several onlookers. She met Shadow and Sondra at the water's edge and grabbed the baby up into her arms. Bernie was crying now too and clung to her leg. She pulled the children up onto the dry sand as Sondra coughed and sputtered. Finally, getting a good breath, the child wailed loudly.

By now, people had gathered around, astonished at the dog's heroic efforts, petting and praising her profusely.

Shadow rather enjoyed the attention and sat grinning at them with her tongue hanging out. She had many people ready to throw her stick that day and went home exhausted.

Meanwhile, the grateful Golda had called the newspaper to report what had happened. The next day, a reporter appeared on the beach with a photographer and took several pictures of Shadow.

The story appeared in the Western World, with pictures of Shadow and of the mother and child. Shadow's picture was taken with Mavis too, whose name was included in the story. The Coos Bay Times, then the Portland papers picked up the story. Then it was broadcast on TV. Shadow was a town hero.

Several days later, Shadow's original owners called to tell Mavis that they had seen the news reports and were anxious to get their dog back.

By now, Mavis thought of Shadow as her dog, as did the entire town. She frowned, fiddled with her apron strings. Maybe they didn't have proof of ownership. Finally, she told them if they could prove they were her owners, she would hand Shadow over.

The next weekend Mavis heard the dogs barking and raising a ruckus as a strange couple knocked on her door. When she opened it, she saw a thin, mousey, sixtyish woman in jeans and a hooded sweatshirt standing next to a portly, bespectacled, balding man, also in jeans and a sweatshirt. They smiled effusively and chorused, "Hi. We're the Wheatlands. We came for Sally."

Mavis gave them a blank stare. "Sally?"

"Yes. You know. Our dog. I believe you call her 'Shadow.' Her real name is Sally."

Mavis' heart sank. "Um. Oh yes! You mentioned that on the phone. I guess you'd better come in."

They followed her into her spotless kitchen. She turned. "Please, have a seat. Can I get you a cup of tea or coffee?"

The couple remained standing. "We'd really just like to see Sally and get her home, if you don't mind. We have a long drive back." Mavis was put off by this unsociable answer. She didn't trust these people and would have liked to learn more about them.

"Where do you live?"

"Up east of Eugene, in Jarvis."

"That's a long drive. I can see why you're in a hurry. I do have to ask you for proof that the dog is yours, though. I've grown very fond of her."

Mrs. Wheatland drew a piece of paper from her purse. "Of course! Here's the receipt from when we bought her from our neighbor. They breed black labs. As you can see, we had her for two years."

She pulled some photos out of her purse. "We have some pictures of us with her when she was a pup. You can see the patch on her chest." Sure enough, the couple were there, proudly holding Shadow. Mavis' heart sank. "We camped at the state park here a year ago, and she went missing. We looked for hours but she just disappeared. We figured someone stole her, since her rope was broken."

Mavis looked glumly at the paper and pictures. They seemed authentic. She sighed. "Did you call the police? Put up signs? Nobody knew where she came from."

"We just figured she was long gone, and we had to get home for appointments," the man piped up. "We were about ready to buy another pup when we saw the report on TV."

Mavis handed back the paper and photos. "Well, these all look good. Why don't you come on out back and see if she recognizes you?"

They followed her out into the yard and, seeing Shadow, called her excitedly. Shadow gave them one look, cowered, and dashed behind the garden shed. Mavis looked at the couple.

"What do you suppose got into her? She obviously knows who you are."

The couple looked flustered. Red-faced, Mr. Wheatland shrugged. "She hasn't seen us for a long time. Maybe she doesn't want to leave her new friends." He indicated the other three dogs, who were watching the scene intently.

Mavis went behind the shed, where she found Shadow trying to dig under the fence. She took hold of Shadow's collar and patted her, talking to her soothingly. "It's all right girl. Your people have come for you. You'll be fine. Come on..." She gently led the resisting Shadow back around to where the couple stood. The man knelt and put his arms firmly around Shadow, murmuring, "Good girl. You're such a good girl." Mrs. Wheatland reached down and primly patted the sleek, black head, babbling baby talk to her. "Oh Sweetie, we missed you sho much, our sugar pie, our baby..." Shadow looked from one to the other but did not look happy. She let out a low whine, tucked her tail between her legs. But she clearly knew who these people were. She looked pleadingly at Mavis.

Mavis admitted to herself that, yes, this was their dog. She had to let her go. She hugged her for the last time and murmured, "I'll miss you, girl. Be happy in your old home."

Shadow stiffened, looked at her longingly, whined as they dragged her into the car. The couple thanked Mavis for taking care of her and got into their car. There was no mention of compensation for her care. They waved and drove off. Mavis looked after them until they turned the corner and were gone. She hadn't liked those people much. They seemed stiff and shifty to her. She told herself that she was just unhappy to let Shadow go. Tears rolled down her cheeks.

Life went on in the town, but many people missed Shadow when they walked on the beach. Mavis hurt when she tucked in her dogs for the night. Four months passed.

Then, one foggy December night, Mavis heard scratching on her door, and a familiar bark. She opened the door and there stood Shadow. Shadow fell forward, crying and licking Mavis' ankles. Mavis half carried her into the house and sat down on the floor with her. Shadow licked her face. "Oh, Shadow. Where have you been? How did you get here?"

The dog was very thin, with her ribs sticking out. Her paws were ragged and scratched, her fur matted. Tears came to Mavis' eyes. The other three dogs were barking joyously and jumping around, nosing Shadow. "Get away, you mutts. Give her room." She half dragged, half carried Shadow into the kitchen and laid her on the small rug she kept in front of the stove. "You rest, baby, and I'll get you food and water."

Shadow stretched out, her chin on her paws and watched as Mavis put food in her bowl and set it in front of her, along with a bowl of water. She lifted her head and began gulping the food down. Then she slurped up the water until it was almost gone. Mabel knelt beside her. She noted a chewed piece of rope still tied around Shadow's neck. She must have been tied up somewhere and broken free. She felt a surge of rage. Those horrible people had taken her lovely dog and tied her up. How had she ever found her way back home? She must have been so starved by the time she got here. She made up her mind that Shadow was never going back. She was hers now.

Shadow slept soundly on her old pad that night. The next day Mavis took her down to see Harry and he looked her over.

"She's got sore paws. She must have been traveling for days, maybe weeks. I can't believe she found her way back here."

Mavis smiled. "It's a miracle. I know one thing. Those people are not getting her back. I think they treated her badly. This is where she belongs." After Harry treated her wounds, she took Shadow home and nursed her back to health.

So, Shadow was soon chasing sticks on the beach again, any time the weather was good enough for people to be out in it. But on cold, blustery winter days, she was content to stay home with her dog friends and Mavis. The townspeople were happy to have her back. Golda and the children visited her every once in a while.

She spent the rest of her life running on the beach, loving Mavis, and playing with her friends. The Wheatlands never came around again. And Mavis didn't advertise Shadow's whereabouts.

When Shadow finally gave in to old age and died, she was buried in the town cemetery and given a lovely headstone of her own. It read, "Shadow, Beloved Hero and Town Dog."

The townspeople and Mavis missed her terribly, but some of them swear they have glimpsed a ghostly black dog, running free on the beach, carrying a stick.

CHAPTER ELEVEN

A LIFE
FORGOTTEN

ALLIE DROVE AROUND the scenic route along the ocean front. The street followed the cliff front that abruptly edged the upper end of the town in the west. It curved south along the cliffs, offering views of the sea to the edge of the world. The great monoliths of stone were incessantly battered by the blue-green waves, sending huge clouds of foam up their sides. This scene always melted Allie's heart, softening the less pleasant memories of her childhood here. Gigantic white clouds sailed over the landscape, allowing the sun to flash through upon the water. The glittering waves calmed down out past the breakers, and far out on the horizon a freighter worked its way south.

They stopped at the parking area on the bluff and watched the sea fling itself at Table Rock, a gigantic, flat topped square of stone, one of the town's favorite landmarks. The wind rushed around the car. It shook the green gorse that covered the cliffsides. The locals call it "Irish Fir." The thorny bushes were actually pretty now, with their brilliant display of bright yellow blossoms.

Allie sighed. "That's the sound I always associate with this town. Always the wind, whistling around the corners.

That, and the sound of the surf. It really is beautiful, though, isn't it?"

"Yeah. I agree about the sounds. I hated the wind."

They watched in silence for a while, lost in memories.

Allie finally started up the car and headed back towards the south jetty. "Let's get out on the beach."

As they turned and drove towards the beach, Allie noticed an empty space between houses. She gestured toward it, eyebrows raised. "Looks like Arnie's shack is gone." She wasn't surprised. Once Arnie was gone, no one else would want to live in it.

Sophie leaned forward. "I see that. Good riddance. It was such an eyesore." Allie steered the car on down to the beach.

ARNIE

Everybody knew old Arnie. He walked miles every day, wearing his olive-green rubber suit and boots when it rained, combing the beach for whatever he could find. He felt sure that someday something wonderful would wash up on the sand, maybe caught behind a twisted driftwood log, maybe stuck in a crack in the rocks. He found lots of glass floats, those much-prized greenish balls that had broken loose from Asian fishnets and floated across the ocean until washed up on shore. He also collected agates, the clear, wave washed stones you could almost see through. Sometimes, if he stared hard, he could see pictures in them. They were used to make cheap jewelry and tourist junk by craftspeople in the area. Arnie had boxes of them stacked on his sagging porch, along with some of the glass balls.

Occasionally, he discovered something someone had dropped or left behind on the beach. He found buckets, coats, hats, shoes and boots, leftovers of lunches and towels. Once he found an unopened six-pack of Hamm's beer, which he enjoyed to the last drop, sitting alone in his ratty recliner in his dark kitchen/living room at night.

His ancient cabin squatted near the beach not far from the south jetty, weathered gray by the wind and salt air, a thick layer of moss covered the roof. He lived alone on his meager social security check. He ate clams, mussels, and seaweed scavenged from the sea. He caught fish from the jetty or the docks. Rumor among the townsfolk had it that he never changed his clothes. When he didn't have on his rain suit, his wiry frame was covered in a ragged gray sweater and heavy black logger's pants and work boots.

People were used to seeing him wandering around town. His neighbors steered clear of him as he emitted a cloud of odious fumes and appeared to be one sandwich short of a picnic. They would have loved to see that old shack go away, but it fought off the wind and rain year after year. Arnie had piles of driftwood stacked around it and a concrete wall in which were embedded many glass balls. The wall was incomplete and, in the end, never finished. His neighbors thought it was hideous and complained to the city about it. A city official came to investigate.

Arnie insisted it was a work of art. "It ain't finished yet. When it's done it'll be great. There ain't no law against it."

The official had to admit that he was right and didn't bother him further.

Arnie didn't have a garage, so his rusting old Chevy pickup sat in the short driveway no matter the weather.

Arnie had his faithful dog, a scruffy, speckled, mournful looking, drooling stray, which also emitted an unpleasant odor. Digger followed him everywhere. He was Arnie's best friend. Sometimes he would sniff out a find on the beach, such as a leftover sandwich.

When Arnie was about seventy-five, one day, he and Digger were poking around a remote area of the beach. People didn't generally walk as far as he did, away from the access roads. He knew the ten miles of coastline south of the jetty intimately. Digger ran ahead of him, investigating all the nooks and crannies. That day, Digger ran up to a bleached and twisted driftwood log that lay partially buried in the sand at the base of the cliff. He jumped over the log, sniffed around, and began pawing the sand.

Arnie walked up to investigate. Digger rummaged frantically at something wrapped in a plastic bag, that had been buried in a deep hole behind the log. Arnie pushed Digger aside and began excavating the bag. It looked like a regular, black garbage bag. He finally pulled it out from its hiding place. It was heavy. Inside the plastic bag, was a fisherman's tacklebox. Arnie felt a thrill go all the way up his spine. He quickly looked around to see if anyone was in the area to claim it. The beach lay deserted. His excitement growing, he tried to open the box, but it was locked. He decided to take it home and pry it open there. He patted Digger. "Good boy, Digger. I've gotta feelin' that this might be our treasure at last." He tucked it under his arm and headed for home.

Back in his house, Arnie cleared a space on his cluttered kitchen table and set the bag down. He found a screwdriver and went to work. He finally managed to spring the lock and opened the lid. He gasped and stepped back from it. He had never seen so much money in his life. The box was full of stacks of money, maybe thousands of dollars. He sat down abruptly. His mind whirled. "My treasure. At last, my treasure. Jumpin' Josephat!" Joy flooded his whole body. His heart raced and his face split in a huge grin. He looked at Digger. "Look, boy, we're rich. Hallelujah!" He jumped up and whirled around in a little jig, with Digger barking and jumping in his wake.

Digger had never seen Arnie this animated. His barking finally got to Arnie, and he shushed him. "Digger, I'm gonna buy you the biggest steak I can find. In fact, I'll buy us both one. And I'm goin' to get me some new clothes. And maybe..." His voice faded. He sat there and thought hard. Where did this money come from? It must have been stolen. Whoever buried it there would be back for it. They'd be enraged when they found it was gone. Maybe they were drug dealers. They might kill him.

His excitement cooled. Fear took hold. He jumped up and pulled the shades over all the windows. What if someone had seen him? He'd have to be cagey. Nobody can know what he'd found. Had there been a robbery recently? Maybe he should turn on the radio and listen to the news. He listened intently. Before long the news came on. The lead story was a news bulletin about a bank robbery that had taken place two days previously, in Eugene. A large amount of money had been stolen. The robber was thought to have taken I-5 south, toward California. He sat there, rigid, wondering what to do. Finally, he decided to wait it out. He would lie low and follow the news for several days. For the next three days he never left his house.

Meanwhile, he pulled the box out of the closet, where he'd hidden it. He counted the money. It wasn't just tens and twenties. There were fifty and hundred-dollar bills under the smaller ones. It amounted to $22,000 dollars. He broke out into a sweat. He thought of all the things he could buy with that. Food, beer, new clothes, a truck. A new truck! His old one was barely running. He'd be proud to be seen in a shiny new truck. One that would start first thing when he turned the key. He looked around. He needed a good hiding place. He glanced at the ceiling. There it was. The attic access. It was a square trap door device that pulled down. He counted out one hundred dollars, put them in his pocket, and got out his stepladder. Then he climbed up and pulled down the little door, depositing the tacklebox on the deck inside. Nobody would find it there.

Gradually, as there was no more news of the robbery suspect, he began to relax. That afternoon he left Digger to guard his treasure and went to the grocery store. He loaded up on steaks and frozen French fries and fancy dinner rolls. He bought a pie and a case of his favorite, Hamm's. Then he picked up a local newspaper. He dumped the groceries into the back of his pickup and high-tailed it for home. That night he and Digger feasted well, juicy steaks dribbling grease down their chins. Arnie had two bottles of beer and French fries. He shared the rolls with Digger. His belly stuffed, he saved the pie for later.

Digger gulped down his food and, twenty minutes later, vomited it up. Arnie started to yell at him, but then realized that poor Digger's stomach wasn't used to such fare, and, after all, he did find the money. So, instead, Arnie petted the downcast dog, assuring him that he was, "A good dog. Don't worry about it. I still love ya." Then he cleaned up the mess without complaint.

He searched the paper for clues about the money. There was a short article about the bank robbery. The thief had absconded with a large amount of cash. Police were asking for any help the public could give them about the robbery. Arnie sat up, frowning. He decided that must be where the money came from. Maybe the robber would be looking for him. He'd better lie low. It occurred to him that he should call the police, but hell no. Finder's keepers!

Arnie stayed away from the beach for a couple of weeks. Instead, he did a little shopping here and there. He went up to Coos Bay where nobody knew him and bought some new jeans and sweatshirts and even splurged on underwear and socks. Then new boots and a warm, red, waterproof winter jacket. He couldn't remember the last time he'd bought any clothes. Looking at himself in the mirror he decided that the coat made him look very respectable. He puffed out his chest.

He hauled his booty home, then cleaned the junk out of his old bathtub, which was full of old bottles and cans. He scrubbed it clean, then filled it and had a long, luxurious soak. He even washed his hair and beard. He'd forgotten what that felt like. Almost like he had new skin. After that, he donned a completely new outfit from the skin out. It felt really good, if a little stiff. He burned his old clothes in his wood stove. He tried to see what he looked like in the wavy bathroom mirror. He peered in closely, then backed off to get a fuller view. "Damn. I look great. A reg'lar Clark Gable. Fine and dandy. The ladies will look at me now, won't they Digger?" He looked wistfully at his image in the mirror.

His eyes glistened. "Wish Ida could see me now. She'd be sorry she left, wouldn't she?"

He was never quite sure why Ida married him. He'd thought she was wonderful, even if she drank too much. He was a lonely, twenty-five-year-old orphan with few friends when he met Ida in the pub. She was thirty, but she was plump and juicy and led him on. No woman had ever paid that much attention to him since his mother died when he was fifteen. He had a steady job at the service station, pumping gas, and he owned the house he'd inherited. She seemed impressed with that.

After they were married, she urged him to put her name on his small savings account, and the checking account. Over time, she started calling him "Dummy," and criticizing everything he did. He couldn't please her no matter how he tried. Once, he'd bought her a bright pink dress he thought was pretty. She unwrapped the package excitedly, looked at the dress, and frowned. "Arnie, you know I don't look good in pink. I look good in blues and greens and reds. Take it back."

It seemed to go that way whenever he did anything he thought would make her happy. After a few months, she made him sleep on the sofa, claiming that his snoring kept her awake.

Meanwhile, she bought expensive clothes and things for the house. Their checking account started coming up short at the end of the month. The marriage lasted less than a year. Maybe if he'd had more money then she'd have stuck around. As it was, she cleaned out his bank account and left town with a traveling Kirby salesman. A tear coursed down Arnie's cheek. He had been alone ever since. Except for Digger.

At least he had him. He sighed and went to put together some scrambled eggs and bacon for the two of them. Digger padded along behind, always attuned to Arnie's moods.

Two days later, Arnie walked into the local Ford sales lot. Harold Wilson popped out of his office. He didn't even recognize Arnie at first.

"Can I help you?"

Arnie flashed his gap-toothed grin. "Hi, Harry."

Harold stepped back. His hackles rose. It was Arnie, the town bum. What was he doing here? His nose wrinkled.

Arnie didn't notice. "I'd like to get a new pickup, Harry. I was lookin' at that blue one over there."

Harold's eyebrows shot up. "I don't think you can afford that, Arnie. It's this year's model."

"Yeah. Well, I had a bit of luck." Arnie looked at Harold sidewise. "My aunt died and left me some money. So, I'm getting a new truck."

Harold was practically in a state of shock. He eyed Arnie skeptically. "Are you sure you've got enough?"

Arnie frowned at the salesman. He knew he wasn't very smart, but he could sense when someone was looking down on him. "I'm sure. What'll you give me for my Chevy?"

Wilson stammered. "I, um, we probably couldn't give you anything for that, Arnie."

"Well, I don't want it. Can you junk it for me? I'll pay cash for that-there blue truck if you'll do that."

Still skeptical, Harry looked into Arnie's rheumy eyes. "It's $1,577, Arnie. You sure you can afford it?"

Arnie snapped, "If you'll take in my Chevy, I'll pay you cash. Do you want to make a sale or not?"

Astonished, Wilson backed up a step, gulped, and said, "In that case, I think we could do it."

Harry was shocked when Arnie handed him a paper sack with $2,000 in it. The deal was signed right away. Arnie drove off in his shiny new pickup. And with change in his pocket.

Word got around town about Arnie paying cash for a new truck. People began speculating.

Arnie went up to Coos Bay a couple of days later and bought himself a new, twelve-foot aluminum fishing boat with a 7.5 horsepower outboard motor and a hitch and trailer for his truck. He hauled it home that very day. He turned on the radio, loud, to his favorite country music, tapping his fingers to the beat, grinning at Digger. "Now we can fish in the river like the other guys. We're goin' ta catch them big salmon, Digger. You'll see."

That evening, Arnie decided to eat out at a local pub, and enjoy a few beers with some of the guys who hung out there. He put on his new jacket and boots and his new-found confidence, and walked into the "Pub 'n Grub," a slightly seedy place on the edge of town. One of the local fishermen, Ron Allen, stared at him in mid-bite as he sat at the bar. "Arnie, I ain't seen you lookin' so dressed up and clean in the forty years I've known you. What's happened? Did ya win the lottery?" This got the attention of the other four men at the bar, especially the stranger sitting on the end stool. They all stared at him.

Arnie ordered a Hamm's, and answered nervously, "Well now, my aunt died and left me some money. Thought I'd get cleaned up a bit."

Ron whistled. "Wow, Arnie. That's great! Is that where you got the dough for the new pickup?" There were murmurs of congratulations along the line of stools. One of the fishermen grumbled, "You must have hit it big."

Arnie shifted uneasily on his feet. "Um, yeah. She was pretty well off and didn't have no family."

A stranger, sitting at the bar, looked at Arnie intently. Arnie ordered a hamburger and fries and sat down at a booth in the corner. The stranger chatted with Ron a bit and picked up his glass. He meandered casually over to Arnie's table.

"Hi, Arnie. Congratulations on your good luck." He held out his hand. "I'm Tom Tate. Mind if I join you?"

Arnie ignored the hand and eyed him suspiciously. The guy was wearing a fishing vest over a plaid shirt and jeans. He looked too spiffy to Arnie. "What for?"

The man smiled, revealing a missing tooth. "Well, your friend, Ron, over there was telling me what a fine fisherman you are and I thought you might give me some clues as to where would be the best place to fish around here."

Arnie was flattered. "Oh. Okay. Sit. Git a load off."

Tate slid into the booth across from Arnie.

"I got places that're my secret spots, so I don't tell nobody where those are. But I can give you some hints as to what bait works best and where most of the locals do their fishin.'"

Again, the ingratiating smile. "I'd really appreciate it. Can I buy you a beer?"

Arnie's eyes registered surprise and he glanced away at the bar. "It's your money, I guess. Make it a Hamm's."

The stranger signaled the barman and smiled as he brought over two more bottles. They talked fishing for a while as Arnie's food was delivered and he gulped it down with huge bites. As they talked, the stranger ordered two more rounds of beer, and soon they were good buddies.

"Well, Arnie, I'd really appreciate it if you could give me a fishing lesson. I've fly-fished in ponds and creeks, but never in the ocean or an actual river."

Arnie hesitated. "Um, I guess we could go out tomorrow morning with my new boat. I'm anxious to try it on the river. Maybe get a salmon."

"That'd be great. Where should I meet you? What time?"

"Um, well, you could meet me at my house. Five-thirty. I go out early."

"Okay. I'm stayin' at the Seaside Motel. Give me your address and I'll be there at 5:30 sharp."

"Don't need no address. Ya can't miss it. It's got a concrete wall part way around it and my blue pickup and boat in the driveway. It's on the flat area down near the south jetty."

Arnie finished up his beer and fries. He got up tipsily, steadying himself on the back of the booth. "See ya in the mornin.'"

The stranger swallowed the rest of his beer and left too.

A few days later, one of the local fishermen found Arnie's boat, hung up on shore where it was caught in an eddy. There was no sign of Arnie or Digger. His trailer was found in the parking area near the boat ramp. His pickup was missing. Big Al decided to go and check out Arnie's place. He knocked on the door of the shack several times and received no reply. He tried the door, found it unlocked, and walked in.

"Arnie," he yelled. "You here?" No reply. He looked through the bedroom situated off the living room. The bed had been torn apart; clothes strewn about. Dresser drawers were pulled out and the contents spilled all over. He checked the tiny, grubby bathroom, then the living room/

kitchen area. The place was a mess. Much messier than he had expected, even for an old bachelor, with furniture ripped up and dishes piled in the sink of the greasy kitchen. The cupboards had all been opened and the contents pulled out on the floor. Someone had been looking for something. He noticed that the hatch in the ceiling had been left open. He pulled up a stepstool and shone his flashlight into the attic. It looked like a trail of dust marked where something had been dragged out. Al stepped back. What had happened to Arnie? There wasn't any blood anywhere that he could see, so no sign of violence other than the mess.

He walked around the outside of the house. Nothing seemed out of the ordinary. But Arnie's pickup was gone, the fabled blue pickup that everyone was talking about. Al shook his head in bewilderment. He checked with Arnie's neighbors, but none of them had seen him. One neighbor reported seeing a strange man come to Arnie's house very early several days earlier but couldn't describe him. Al headed back to the office.

Al called in the county sheriff for help in searching for Arnie, and the river was searched and dragged near where the boat was found. But no trace of him or Digger was found. Al knew there had been foul play but didn't know exactly what. In asking around Arnie's favorite haunts, he learned about the stranger who had taken such an interest in Arnie a few nights before. He had come into town, spent a few nights at the Seaside Motel, signed the register as "Tom Tate." They did find his car parked around the corner from Arnie's place. He left no sign of ownership on or in it, no fingerprints. But a trace on the license plate revealed that it had been stolen.

Al put out an APB on Arnie's truck and on "Tom Tate." The truck was found a week later, parked on a side street in Eugene. Tom Tate was never found.

Arnie and Digger were also never found. Rumors abounded. He had been seen walking on the beach south of town. He had taken off with his new friend. He had been murdered and fed to the sharks. What had happened to Digger? He would never leave Arnie's side. It was a mystery, and a source of unending speculation. Finally, people concluded that Arnie and Digger had been drowned and washed out to sea.

They held a memorial for him at the First Southern Rite Holy Baptist Church of Christ. A few of the townspeople came, feeling guilty for the way they had avoided him. As the service progressed, they realized that very few people really knew the man. Long ago, the story went, he had a wife, who left him for a traveling salesman. He had no family, and only a few casual acquaintances. It was like he had always just been there. After his wife left, he became reclusive. The pastor struggled to give a eulogy for a man he didn't know. Mostly he talked about love and caring for our neighbors, even the difficult ones. The people resumed their lives and the speculation about him eventually faded into history. Years later his shack was bulldozed away.

Allie and Sophie spent the rest of the morning enjoying the beach and watching the fishing boats going in and out. Then, they went back to the waterfront in search of a good seafood lunch. They didn't think about Arnie's blank lot as they drove past.

CHAPTER TWELVE

THE RANCH

THE NEXT DAY, after a hearty breakfast, Allie steered the car on along the waterfront. She glanced at Sophie. "Wanna drive out past the old home place and take a look? I'll bet I haven't been by there in fifteen years."

"Let's do it. I'd like to see how much of it's still standin'. We don't have to hurry back for anything. We can stay another day or two."

"I'm game. This is the closest thing to a vacation I've had in ages."

They continued on across the bridge and out the ten miles of the twisting road where they had grown up. Allie remembered the long, dusty, bumpy rides from their home, ten miles of potholed gravel to town, to school, to church, to any event that called for the trip. Now it was paved, a big improvement. There were more houses strung along the way, where before there had been only forests and brush. As they came to what their parents had called "The Ranch," even though it had only been a few acres of land, they were shocked. The old house was gone. They weren't even sure it was the same place.

"Where'd it go? There's nothing here," exclaimed Sophie.

"Maybe it just rotted away. Maybe somebody tore it down to build a new house there."

Sophie's face fell. "It's like our childhoods have disappeared." Her voice caught in her throat. "Mama and Daddy built that house from nothing, all by themselves."

Allie stared at the empty space. She was lost in remembrance. The little house that was home to their family of eight had no bathroom, just an outhouse, no phone, no running water, and was never finished the whole time they lived there. It perched on wood pilings on the gently sloping piece of land. The back porch opened into the kitchen and was the only door they ever used since the front steps had never been built to the elevated front door. It was surrounded by trees back then. Now there was nothing but brush. A feeling of sadness enveloped her as she remembered the worst thing that ever happened to the family in their history there.

ALICIA

Alicia wriggled her body to find a more comfortable spot in her "climbing tree." She loved the smooth bark of this alder tree and its fresh, sharp smell. This was her favorite hiding/reading place when the weather was nice. Once away from her crowded house she could read to her heart's content without being disturbed by her numerous brothers and sisters, or her mother wanting her to do chores. Alone in her tree she had her own little world where she could relax. No one telling her, "Go outside and play. Get your nose out of your book."

Today she was deeply engrossed in an Edgar Rice Burroughs book, Tarzan of the Apes. While she didn't believe for a minute that a baby could survive in the jungle, raised by a gorilla, she loved the idea anyway. She was lost in imagining life in the jungle when she heard a voice from the ground far below.

"Allie, Mom says you need to come help get supper on."

Allie was startled, and nearly dropped her book. "It's early yet. I'll come in a few minutes."

"No," yelled Matthew. "She wants you to come now."

"All right," she snapped. "Go away. I'll be down in a minute. I need to finish this page."

"You're gonna be in trouble. She's gonna be mad. Don't say I didn't warn you." At age nine, Matthew, three years younger than Allie, relished the idea of seeing his sister in trouble.

"Just go away."

He turned and stomped off. She knew he was right. She was always getting into trouble for "wasting her time" reading. But it was the only thing that kept her sane, living in this isolated place. She sighed heavily, marked her page, and slapped her book shut. Slowly, she worked her way back to earth and everyday life.

She followed the trail back to the house, angrily kicking clods of dirt as she went. Her tree was in the back acreage of their property, down a trail her father had bushwhacked through the thick brush. Too soon she was on the porch and clomped up the steps to the kitchen. *Sometimes,* she thought, *I wish I lived all by myself and I could read all I wanted to.*

Her mother, Rose, was already there, placing the chicken in the frying pan. It sizzled as she dropped each piece in.

She snapped at Alicia, "Allie, where have you been? I need you to peel the potatoes and get them on to boil. I can't do everything."

Allie muttered, "Okay, Mama. Sorry." She tucked her book away on a shelf in the living room, returned to the kitchen, and grabbed the peeler from the drawer of kitchen gadgets. She bellied up to the counter and began peeling at a furious pace. As soon as she had a pot full of potato chunks, she poured water on them and set them on the stove.

Her mother's black hair was moist around her face from working over the hot stove. She spoke less sharply. "Thanks, Allie. Now, would you wash the lettuce for the salad? I got a nice bunch from the garden this afternoon." She proceeded to put the green beans on to boil.

Allie hated washing the lettuce. She always got her sleeves wet, and it took forever. But it had to be done so she did it. Soon, she had a bowl full of wet lettuce. "All done."

"Okay. Thanks, Allie. Now pile it in that clean dishtowel, gather up the corners and take it out and swing it around to get the water out of it."

Allie complied. It was kind of fun swinging the "bag" of lettuce and watching the spray dampen the ground. Finally, she took it in and emptied the leaves into a bowl. Following Rose's instructions, she tossed together a salad, then drained the potatoes and mashed them. Sophie, who was ten, set the table. Together they soon had the evening meal on the table for all to gather around.

Sitting at the table, Allie surveyed her six siblings and her parents. There was Caleb, sixteen, skinny and tall, and Albert, fourteen, just beginning to grow out of his chubbiness, and the four younger ones, Sophie, ten, Matthew, nine, four-year-old Caroline and Lilly, eighteen months. Her pretty Mama sat at one end of the table, and Daddy at the other. Allie thought her father was very handsome, with his shock of black hair and his rugged face. It was nice to have everyone in one place together. They all bowed their heads and said grace. That done, they quickly dove into the food.

Lilly was the family pet, and everyone adored her, even the older boys, who enjoyed playing with her. She had big blue eyes and light sandy hair, unlike her dark haired, brown eyed siblings. Her father joked that she was a "throwback." She sat in the highchair and banged her spoon randomly on her tray. Allie smiled at her and quickly put potatoes and gravy in her bowl, and some green beans. Allie never minded taking care of Lilly, even changing her diapers.

Lilly looked at her listlessly and poked at her food. Her mother frowned. "She's just been off her feed today. Been fussy too. She's had this cold for a couple of days now. I hope she gets over it soon."

Allie watched her while she ate her own dinner. Yes, Lilly wasn't acting normally. Her nose was runny, and her eyes were rather red. She felt a spark of worry.

The children mostly ate in silence while their parents caught up on the news of the day. Allie was always fascinated by her father's hands as she sat across from him. They were large and gentle, with tough calluses, stained by the hand rolled cigarettes he smoked. He was not a demonstrative man but would occasionally pat his children on the head with those big hands or give them a hug. He was slow moving and soft spoken unless he was angry, which didn't happen often. But when it did, watch out. She had felt the sting of one of those hands smacking her backside a couple of times when she was sassy or disobedient.

Her parents discussed the day's events. Sometimes her father had an interesting tale to tell about his adventures. He drove the road-grader for the county, smoothing out the gravel roads that wended through the countryside. There weren't many paved roads in Coos County in the 50s. Sometimes the conversation would veer into politics. Allie always felt her stomach tighten when the talk of possible nuclear war with the Russians came up. Some people were actually building bomb shelters. Her parents scoffed at that. "What good would it do to survive an attack if everyone else was killed? Or if everything was contaminated with radioactivity? Allie wondered that too. She concentrated on her food.

Allie and Sophie had to do the dishes after dinner and there was always a dispute about whose turn it was to wash. Allie preferred to wash, as the drier also had to put the dishes away. That always took longer. There were a lot of dishes and pots and pans to do. She hated it. But once they got at it, it didn't usually take more than half an hour or so. The procedure required draining the water tank on the big old wood cook stove into the dishpans, to get the hot water needed. Then they had to refill the tank from the water buckets. (Allie detested the fact that they had no plumbing in this house, like her town classmates did. She did her best to never let the "townies" know that they didn't have an indoor bathroom.) The boys would have to go out and pump the buckets full again at the well in the yard.

The boys helped their father in the barn. They fed the calf and the chickens and cleared the barn floor, throwing down fresh straw. Their dad did the milking and saw to Bessy, their sweet-tempered Jersey cow. The boys did most of the wood chopping for the endlessly consuming cook stove and the heater in the dining room.

Allie was glad she didn't have to work in the stinky barn and hen house. She much preferred the inside chores. However, on occasion, when needed, she could chop wood too and actually enjoyed it. Or, rarely, she could chop the head off of a chicken for dinner. She thought the cleaning process was gross, but her mother did most of that.

When the chores were done, the older children convened in the yard and spent the early evening playing "Kick the Can." It was fun to play as darkness fell because they could hide more easily in the dark. Home base, the empty can, was in the center of the bare dirt yard. Allie found it exhilarating to dash in and kick the can in the dark before the person who was "it" could beat her. If she lost, she was "it." If she won, the person who was "it" retained the title.

Finally, mother called the children in to get ready for bed and say their prayers. The boys shared one room with bunk beds. Allie shared a room with Sophie, Caroline and Lilly. The three older girls slept in a double bed together. It was crowded, but at least they were never cold. Lilly had a crib in the corner.

Sometimes, when the others were asleep, Allie would pull out a flashlight and read under the covers. Not tonight, though. She was too tired. She listened to the frogs croaking in the boggy area near the road that ran by their house. They were very noisy in the spring. She loved the sound of their chorus. They almost drowned out her other favorite sound, the roar of the ocean surf in the distance. Before she had quite dropped off, her mother tiptoed into the room. She checked on Lilly and pulled up her cover. She whispered to

Allie, "I'm worried about Lilly. She still seemed listless after dinner and has a little fever. If she wakes up, you come get me right away."

Allie whispered back, "Okay, Mama." Her concern for her little sister made it difficult to doze off but she finally managed it.

She was awakened from a deep sleep by the sudden sound of Lilly, crying and coughing a deep, vibrating cough. She jumped out of bed and picked the child up, feeling her forehead. She was very hot. She barely had time to cry between coughs. Before she could go to fetch her mother, she was there. "Allie, what's happening? Why is she crying?"

"I don't know. She just started crying and she has a terrible cough."

Her mother took the baby in her arms, her forehead deeply creased with worry. "I'll go get the thermometer. You can go back to bed, Allie. Thank you for getting her."

Allie sat on the edge of her bed, but she didn't get in. She could hear Lilly in her distress as her mother tended to her in the dining room. Soon, she heard them go into her parent's room and her mother and father discussing something urgently.

Allie got up, put on her robe and slippers, and went out to the living room to wait. She was very frightened. Soon, her parents emerged from their room, fully dressed. They had Lilly wrapped in a warm blanket.

Her mother saw Allie waiting there, her eyes big with fear. "Allie, we're taking Lilly to the doctor. I think she may have whooping cough."

Allie just sat there, mute and terrified. Her father went in to get Caleb and brought him out into the living room.

"Okay, Caleb and Allie, I'm counting on you to take care of things until we get back. Wake the kids up and get them fed and dressed for school. Caleb, you take the alarm clock into your room. Take care of the animals and all of you get off on the bus in the morning. It might be quite a while before we get back."

Allie pressed her fist against her mouth. She had never been so frightened. Lilly couldn't stop coughing and was wheezing terribly. She looked at her father. "Can I stay here until you get home? I can't go to school when I'm so worried about Lilly. Besides, someone has to stay here with Caroline."

He paused. "That's right. I almost forgot; I'm not thinkin' clear. You and Caleb can stay home to take care of Caroline and take care of things here. The rest should go to school."

Allie was crying by now, and Caleb's face reflected the fear they were all feeling. He looked at his father, squared his shoulders, saying, "We'll take care of things here, Dad. Don't you worry."

His father patted his shoulder. "That's my good kids. We've got to hurry. Try to get some more sleep."

With that, their parents rushed out the door with Lilly. Allie and Caleb looked at each other. "I'm so scared, Caleb. She's really sick."

"The doctor'll know what to do. We just have to hold down the home front. She'll be all right. Go back to bed." But she could see that he was scared too, by the way his forehead wrinkled, and he hunched his shoulders, his hands balled into fists.

Allie shuffled back to her room, still crying. She knew she wouldn't get any more sleep. It was ten miles to the nearest doctor. What if Lilly died? Her cough was awful.

Why hadn't she woken up sooner to take care of her? She wiped her face on her sleeve and took off her robe. She slipped into bed. A worried little voice said, "Allie, is Lilly okay?" It was Sophie.

"Where's Lilly?" chimed in four-year-old Caroline. Both girls were sitting up. Sophie started to cry, then Caroline took it up. Allie put her arms around them.

"I'm sure she's goin' to be fine. Mama and Daddy are takin' her to the doctor so he can help her. Lay down and go back to sleep."

The girls finally stopped sniffling and lay back down. They huddled close together. The two little ones finally closed their eyes and slipped into sleep. Allie lay there, wide-awake, until the morning light came in through the window.

She slid out of bed, quietly got dressed, and went into the kitchen. She carefully started a fire in the range, then stoked the coals in the heater, feeding them wood chips until they caught fire and then adding larger chunks of wood. At least the house would be warm when the kids woke up.

She put on a pot of water to boil and measured out the oatmeal. Then methodically set the table for breakfast, sliced bread for toast and sandwiches, and put the milk pitcher on the table. When the oatmeal was done, she set it on the back of the stove to keep it warm. As she made the toast, the fragrance reminded her that she hadn't eaten. All the while, the hard ball of fear seemed to lodge itself in her chest. Looking at the clock, she realized that it was time to wake everyone up for school.

She went in and woke Sophie, helped her pick out a dress for school, and returned to the kitchen. While Sophie got dressed she packed lunches for the school children. The alarm went off in the boys' room. She heard Caleb get up and rouse the younger boys. His voice was low as he told the younger boys what had happened, and she heard their shocked exclamations. Soon Caleb came out. The boys dressed quickly and ran to the outhouse. It was a long ride to school.

The children gathered glumly around the dining table. Caroline shuffled sleepily out of her room and joined them. Allie and Caleb led them in the grace, and then they prayed for Lilly. They gamely ate what they could. They were unnaturally quiet. Usually, there was a lot of noise and bickering around the breakfast table. When they were finished, the older ones helped the younger ones put on their coats and gather school bags and lunch sacks. While Caleb went out to do the chores, Allie watched the clock so she could send the children out to the bus on time.

Allie and Caroline waved good-bye to the children when they boarded the bus and slowly returned to the house. Caroline played quietly with her dolls while Allie cleaned up the breakfast mess. Then the two of them sat down while Allie read several of Caroline's favorite Dr. Seuss books to her. Caroline was subdued and clung close to Allie. "When's Mommy and Daddy comin' home? Is Lilly okay?"

Allie stifled her worry, trying to reassure Caroline. "I'm sure they'll be home soon. The doctor should fix Lilly up just fine. Don't you worry."

Time dragged by, as Allie watched the clock and strained to hear the family car returning. The sound of a car crunching down the gravel road made her heart race, and she jumped up, straining to see. But it was only one of the neighbors. She felt acutely disappointed as he drove on by. This was one of the times when she felt really angry about the fact that they lived beyond the reach of the telephone lines.

Caleb came in from his chores, placed a bucket of eggs on the counter, and went into his room. Allie put the eggs in the refrigerator and tried to think of a game to play with Caroline. Finally, she sat in the rocker and rocked the child, who eventually dozed off. Allie took her to their room and laid her on the bed, covering her with the blanket. Time dragged while Caroline slept. Allie looked for things to do. She swept the floor and tidied the living room. She picked up her book but couldn't concentrate. After reading the same line three times, she set it aside. When Caroline woke up, she went into their room, made the bed and tidied it up. The knot in her stomach seemed to be growing.

Caleb emerged from his room and went outside. She heard the axe as he splintered firewood with loud whacks. He worked at it until lunchtime. When he came in, she had peanut butter sandwiches waiting for him and milk. The three of them ate in silence, each walled in with worry. Only once did Caleb break the silence. He looked at Allie and said, "She'll be all right. She has to. We got to think positive." Allie nodded but couldn't finish her sandwich.

When Caroline was finished, Allie helped her clean up and put her coat on her. She slipped into her own coat, and they went for a walk down the gravel country road. They walked up to the top of the hill west of the house to Allie's favorite viewing/thinking spot. Sitting in the grass on the knoll beside the road, she could see all the way to the ocean. The scene below was lovely and peaceful. The road curved around the top of the hill and took a dive to the floor of the little valley below, and then wound its way up the equally steep hill on the other side. A lovely stream ran through the middle of the valley to the sea. Alley could spend hours just sitting there in her quiet spot, watching the waves roll in over the gray sand, thinking and dreaming. Today, she prayed for Lilly and begged God to save her. "I'll never complain about my chores again if you'll just make her well," she whispered.

Caroline was less contemplative, and spent a few minutes playing in the grass, inspecting the plants and watching bugs as they busily scurried on their errands. She studied the water flowing in the roadside ditch and sent seedpod boats floating down the hill. After about twenty minutes she was ready to go home. Allie reluctantly tore herself away and holding the child's warm little hand, led her back to the house.

Finally, in mid-afternoon, Allie heard the family car pull into the yard. She raced to the door, flew through it and down to where her father was getting out of the car, with Caleb close on her heels. Their father's face was unsmiling.

"Where's Mama? What's wrong with Lilly? Will she be okay?"

He put his arm around her and guided her back to the house. "Lilly has whooping cough. She's in the hospital and the doctor's taking care of her. Your mother stayed with her so she wouldn't be scared. I'm afraid we'll have to get along without her for a few days."

He picked up Caroline, who was standing on the porch. "After dinner, I'll pack your mother's things and take them to her, so she has a change of clothes and whatnot." He looked at Allie. "I'm sorry, Honey. We all have to pray for your baby sister." His voice trembled a bit when he said that.

Allie asked faintly, "Is she gonna die?"

"They're doin' all they can for her. It's serious, but I think she'll pull through with God's help. We have to be positive."

Slowly they trekked into the familiar warmth of the little house. Her father sat down in the rocking chair, his face pale and drained. "Allie, if I go rest a bit, can you start supper?"

"Okay, Daddy. I got some hamburger out of the freezer so I can make some Spanish rice. I know how to do that."

He smiled weakly. "I knew I could count on you. Good girl. Once I've rested a bit I'll get at the milking. I want to head back to town as soon as we're done eating."

He got up, patted her on the shoulder, and slowly walked into his bedroom. Caleb wandered back outside, and she soon heard the whack of the axe hitting wood.

Allie felt proud that Daddy trusted her with the responsibility of making dinner, but she couldn't stop thinking about Lilly. She missed her mother too. She looked at the clock. The kids would be arriving back home soon. She would have to entertain Caroline until then, when Sophie could take over while she fixed dinner. She took out Caroline's little China tea set and placed it on a tea towel on the floor. "Let's have a tea party, Caroline. Would you like that?"

"Yay," the child crowed. "Can we have sandwiches too?"

"Let's see what we can find for a snack with our tea."

Together they found an apple, which Allie sliced, and made tiny peanut butter and cracker sandwiches. They knelt on the floor with their snacks, and Caroline ceremoniously poured her "tea" into tiny cups. They carried on a ladylike conversation, pretending to be princesses, as they sipped and munched. "And what have you been doing lately, Princess Caroline"

"Oh, I walked in the garden and went to a big ball last night."

"Oh, my, that must have been delightful"

Allie thought that chubby, pretty Caroline, with her big brown eyes and dark, curly hair would make a fine princess. Also, she could be bossy, a proper princess trait. The girls played for another half hour and then cleared up the residue.

Allie was relieved when the rest of the children stepped off the school bus. As soon as they came into the house, Sophie wanted to know if Lilly was okay. Allie told her what her father had said, and Sophie's face fell. The boys listened quietly and then went to their room to change from their school clothes into their chore clothes.

"I need you to watch Caroline while I get dinner on, Sophie. Would you do that?"

"Okay, let me put my stuff away." She turned to her little sister. "Come on, Carrie, let's go in our room." Caroline trailed after her.

Allie busied herself frying the hamburger and putting the rice on to boil. She called to Sophie and Caroline to set the table, and put together a meal of Spanish rice, homemade bread and green beans. Then she woke her father and they all sat down together. It was a quiet dinner and each of them was sunk in his or her own thoughts. The clock ticked loudly in the living room.

Their dad asked how was school that day, and the answers were brief. "Fine." "Okay."

After dinner, Dad went out and milked the cow, and the children did their chores and, for once, there weren't any arguments. Afterwards, their father pulled them all together in the living room. They knelt in a circle, and he led them in prayers for their little sister. Then he rose and informed them that he would be going back into town. "I'm expecting you all to work together and take care of each other and the house while I'm gone. I'll be getting back late so go to bed at the usual time. Allie and Caleb, I've arranged to leave Caroline with your Aunt Verna in town until this is over. Allie, would you pack her a bag to take in the morning? And I want the two of you to go back to school. I'll write your excuses when I get back."

With that, he put on his coat, picked up the suitcase he had packed for their mother, and, after giving each of them a hug, left for town.

Three days dragged by, and still Lilly was sick. The children did their best to carry on. Allie worked to put together passable meals. One night she made pancakes and eggs, another, a noodle and tuna casserole. She spent her spare time studying her mother's Betty Crocker Cookbook.

On the fourth day, Allie's father came to the school at ten o'clock to get the children. He led them out to the car and gathered them around as they looked at each other with dread. Allie was trembling inside. Daddy said, "Kids, I have very sad news. Our Lilly has gone to heaven. Her whooping cough turned into pneumonia and her little body just could not fight it off."

Allie looked at her father, standing there with tears in his eyes, and burst out crying, and the others all followed suit. Daddy comforted them all he could, patting them on their heads and shoulders, murmuring, "It'll be okay. Don't cry. It's okay." He pulled out his big white hanky, mopped their faces, then his own and urged them into the car. He turned around in his seat and explained, "We're going to go to the funeral home now. I want you to be very brave and try not to cry in front of your mamma. She's heartbroken, and we have to do our best to help each other through this."

He took them to the funeral home, where they met their mother and her sister, Verna, and Caroline, all with faces raw from crying. They were escorted into a fancy room, with red velvet drapery on the windows and fancy, gilded couches and chairs. On a low table, in a tiny white coffin, lined with pink satin, lay their darling baby sister. She looked so sweet and peaceful, like she was asleep. But her face was pale and waxen, and she wasn't breathing. Allie choked at the sight of her and couldn't hold back the tears. She didn't think she could bear it. They were going to put her baby sister in the ground. Sophie began to weep, and Allie put her arm around her. She looked at her mother. Her face was frozen in grief. Her eyes and nose were red, and her mouth looked like it would never smile again. Her father stood with his arm around her, clearly fighting to remain calm and strong for them all, his face etched with grief.

Carrie reached up and touched the cold cheek. She began to wail. "I want my Lilly. Bring her back. Bring her back."

Quickly, her father picked her up and carried her out as she sobbed all the way. Mama looked like she was going to faint, and suddenly sat down on the plush, velvet chair placed nearby. Their Aunt Verna was by her side and put her arm around her.

Mama looked at the children and gestured for them to come close. Putting her arm around Sophie, she told them,

"God has decided that he needs your baby sister more than we do..." her lips trembled, and her voice cracked. She struggled to compose herself and continued, "and has called her home to be with Him." Pause. "We'll all miss her terribly." She struggled to keep her voice calm. "We still have each other, and we must be brave. I know she's smiling down on us from Heaven. We have to leave her now. We'll be back for the rosary and funeral on Saturday." She paused, then, softly, "This is a good time to tell her good-bye."

They all gathered around the coffin. They joined hands and said an "Our Father," then they each took turns, telling her good-bye. Allie, hesitated, then reached down and touched the cold little hand. "Good-bye Lilly," she choked. "I'll miss you so much." She wiped her eyes with her sleeve and turned away. Their aunt led them out to join their father while Mama stayed behind. It seemed that she couldn't bear to leave the baby there, all alone.

Allie lagged behind at the door, reluctant to leave, and watched as her father came back in. He looked at Lilly where she lay and knelt down by her. He bowed his head and prayed for a while, then leaned over and kissed the cold cheek.

Turning to her mama, with tears on his cheeks, Allie watched as he gently urged her to leave with him. Her mother, moving stiffly, her face like stone, reluctantly went out with him.

The family made it through the funeral. Aunt Verna helped with the arrangements and the luncheon afterwards, supplied by the church ladies. Finally, the relatives all left, and the family went back home to their cold house. It seemed empty without Lilly there to amuse them with her antics and her beautiful baby laugh. They all changed into their chore clothes and dispersed silently to their duties. Mother sat in the rocking chair in the living room, rocking Caroline. She seemed stunned and lost.

Allie didn't know what to do. She went out and sought her favorite tree and climbed up into its welcoming branches. She sat there a long time, thinking about Lilly and aching for her. Why hadn't she awakened sooner? Was it her fault that Lilly was dead? Then she thought about her mother. She was hurting more than anyone. What could she do to help her? She decided that she would make dinner for the family. She climbed back down the tree, feeling the smooth bark under her hands, working from limb to limb. She patted the cool trunk and went back into the house. Her mother hadn't moved. Caroline was asleep in her lap.

"Mama, what would you like me to fix for dinner?"

Mama looked at her blankly.

"We have a couple of casseroles that people left. I can warm one of them up and make a salad."

"That would be fine, Allie," came the soft reply. "Thank you."

Allie proceeded to get dinner ready while Sophie set the table. They were out of bread, which their mother usually baked for them. But she figured none of them were very hungry anyway.

After dinner, the older children dawdled over their schoolbooks around the dinner table, and Sophie and Carrie quietly played with their dolls until bedtime.

The days dragged by, and still their mother seemed to be in a trance. When they came home from school she would be sitting in the rocker, staring out of the window, or holding Caroline and rocking her with her eyes closed.

She let the housework go, and Allie tried to take up the slack. She swept the floors and pushed the other children to help tidy things. On Saturday, her father and Caleb hauled water to the washing machine on the back porch, helped her start the engine, and she tried to do a passable job on the laundry. That evening, they heated the water for their baths, and she made sure the younger ones got themselves clean in the old wash tub, before she took her own bath in the same water. The older boys took care of themselves. She managed to scrape together meals and kept a grocery list so her father could get groceries on his way home from work. They were buying bread now, since their mother didn't seem to have the energy to make it anymore. They ate a lot of peanut butter and jelly sandwiches for lunch.

Allies' grades began to fall, and she was exhausted all the time. She felt overwhelmed with taking care of her family and worrying about her mother.

Her father was suffering too, and never smiled. He yelled at Albert for not cleaning out the chicken house properly. He had almost never yelled at the children before. He was gentle with her mother for a long time, and tried to urge her to resume life as it was before. He cajoled her, "Rose, you're being unfair to the kids and me. Allie is taking on all the housework and looking after the little ones and trying to do her studies. You have six living children who need you..." Allie didn't hear the rest of what he said. Her mother murmured a reply she couldn't make out. In this small house with thin walls, it was often easy for the children to hear what their parents said in private. Allie would sometimes hear them talking into the night and sometimes Dad would raise his voice. But nothing seemed to get through to her mother. Her father spent more of his time outdoors or in the barn. Allie knew that he was grieving too.

Another week went by with her mother putting forth minimal effort, dragging through the days. Then one day as the bus pulled up to their stop, Allie leapt off the bus ahead of the other children and tore through the house into her bedroom. She pulled down her panties, looked at them, and screamed, "Mama, come quick. Help me."

Jolted, her mother ran into the room. Allie was looking down at her panties, which she had removed. She looked up, quivering, her face pale. "I'm bleeding, Mama, am I goin' to die?"

Mama was startled. "Oh, Allie. I think you've started your periods. It's okay, Honey, you're not going to die. I'll be right back." She whirled and left the room. Soon she was back with a funny-looking belt and a white pad in her hand.

"Here, Honey, let me show you how to wear this." She proceeded to help Allie into the belt and pad. "This is what you will need to do once every month from now on. When it gets uncomfortably wet, change it for a new one. You've started your menses. You're a woman now, Honey. Here, put on these clean panties and I'll explain all about it."

So, she proceeded to explain the intricacies of menstruation and what Allie needed to do about all this womanly stuff. Allie had heard some of this at school. She had been horrified at the very idea and was determined that it wouldn't happen to her. She cried and declared that she didn't want to do this, she didn't want to be a woman. She was still a kid.

She calmed down as her mother talked. It was the first time since Lilly died that her mother had really come alive.

It was comforting, and she felt the tears of relief sliding down her cheeks. Her mother took her in her arms and Allie let go of all the anguish and misery she had been storing up since the death of her sister.

"Honey, you'll change your mind in time. It's all part of growing up."

She reassured her that she would get used to it. She asked her if she had a tummy ache, and Allie sniffed that, yes, she did. Mama told her to lie down and gave her some aspirin. Then she gave her a warm hot water bottle to hold against her stomach. She sat by Allie on the bed, smoothing her hair, comforting her.

Allie finally let down and cried again. Sobbing, she told her mother that she couldn't do everything anymore. It was too much. She needed her. "I'm sorry Mama. It's my fault Lilly died. I should have heard her sooner and come got you."

"Oh my God, is that what you've been thinking? Oh Baby, it's not your fault. You didn't do anything wrong. The sickness just came on her so fast that we never could have caught it in time. Honey, please believe me, it was never your fault. I had no idea you felt this way." She paused, sniffled. "I've been selfish, wallowing in my own grief. Please forgive me, Allie." She held Allie for a long time and cried some herself. Finally, she told Allie to take a nap, and she'd feel better. Then she got up and went out into the kitchen.

Allie did take a nap and woke up as it was turning dark outside. She got up when she smelled food cooking and went into the kitchen to help her mother get dinner together.

As they all sat around the table that evening, they said grace, and added a prayer for Lilly. Then Mama looked at her family and, with a tremulous smile, said, "I want to tell you all that I'm sorry I've been so withdrawn. I just want you to know that I'm better now and will be here for you whatever happens." She looked at her husband.

Daddy smiled for the first time since Lilly died, his eyes glistening, and settled back in his chair. Mama smiled at him in return. Then she handed a bowl of mashed potatoes to Caleb, who was next to her, and they all began passing the food around. She leaned forward and took them all in. "So how was everybody's day?

The rich bottomland
was soon covered by
wild coastal brush.

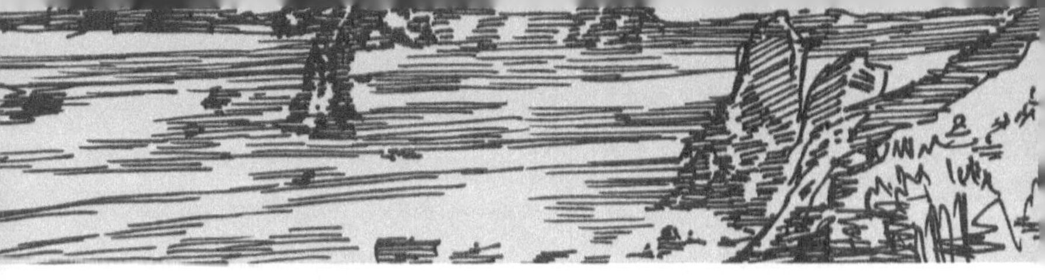

CHAPTER THIRTEEN

THE SELLARS

ALICIA PUT THE CAR IN GEAR and followed the road on up the hill. They passed the spot that had been her special place when she was young—the knoll at the top of the hill with a view of the sea. She had longed to sail on that sea, far away. Maybe to Hawaii or China. To see new and exotic lands. The view had been comforting and relaxing. As they rounded the corner, they could see where the Sellars had lived.

The Sellars owned the land of the north hillsides and the rich bottom land which they used as pasture for their cows. The grass was always green and lush here, fed by the rain and the little stream that flowed out to sea. Their house and barn were long gone, and the land was now a State Park.

When they were young, the Sellars had let them use their rutted farm road out to the wild beach. It was always deserted and free of traffic. It was still deserted today.

"Remember the Sellars?" Alicia asked Sophie. "They were an interesting pair. I was terrified of Gloria Sellars when I was little."

Sophie laughed. "There were rumors that she chased off one of her kids with a butcher knife one time, because he had defied her for some reason. Mom said that she loved children but once they were grown, she lost interest in them. That was weird."

"Yeah. Mom used to make Caleb and me go down there to buy eggs. To me, Gloria looked to be a hundred years old. She had wild gray hair, snared in an untidy bun. She had a loud voice and cackled when she laughed." Allie pictured the woman in her mind. "She dominated her mild-mannered husband, Robert, who basically did what he was told. "Robert, take these young'uns into the house and give'em some cookies." 'Robert, go get those chickens back in the pen.'"

But Mom knew that she wouldn't hurt us. In fact, she and Robert kept us in comic books, and candy. Gloria cared for her nephew—John what's his name? a lot because his mother was ill and indulged him shamefully."

"I remember," Sophie chimed in. "When he was done with the comics, she'd drop off a bundle at our house. I loved those. They kept us entertained all those rainy afternoons and evenings."

"They were good neighbors and would have given us the shirts off of their backs if we needed them. I remember Gloria would show up at our house at least once a week for about six weeks when Lilly was sick and after the funeral. She'd bring casseroles, dressed in her tattered overalls and work boots. All kinds. Macaroni and cheese, tuna and noodle, some weird combinations like garbanzo beans and rice and hamburger."

Sophie chuckled. "I remember that nobody liked the garbanzo beans one."

"Her heart was in the right place. Did you know that Gloria was actually a renowned nurse in our area when she was young? Mama told me not long before she died. She said that doctors would come from miles around to get her to take care of their seriously sick patients. Ya know, doctors used to do house calls in those days." Allie was lost in remembering.

Gloria and Robert had a rustic old house on their farm, that they used for housing their hired hand and his family. One day, that house caught fire. They all fought hard to save it, but it was quickly reduced to ashes. While it was burning, sparks flew over onto the barn, which caught fire also and burned to the ground. Allie saw Robert watching the conflagration with tears running down his cheeks. He loved his barn, but at least the cows were all safely out to pasture.

After that, Gloria decided that it was time to retire. They sold their cows and pretty much let nature take over the place. The rich bottomland was soon covered by wild coastal brush. They also sold off some of their acreage, and thus managed to get by.

It took a while, but Robert got used to being free of the cows, as he kept himself busy with the chickens and the garden they grew. They did some traveling, and hired Caleb to take care of the chickens and their pets when they were gone.

Gloria passed away from breast cancer. Robert was lost for a while, not knowing what to do with himself without Gloria to guide him. Finally, he sold what was left of his property and moved into town. He liked eating at the few restaurants in town and, as time went by, made friends with his neighbors. He kept in touch with his old neighbors too, sometimes driving by and dropping off some candy for the kids.

He grew to like life in town and became a regular at the Laughing Gull Cafe. He lived to be ninety-five, when he passed away in his sleep.

Allie pulled back from reminiscing about her childhood. "Let's drive on down to the park and walk on the beach."

They pulled on their hats and jackets and walked for an hour on the cold, gray sand, listening to the surf and the gulls as they sailed overhead. Allie couldn't help but notice how much the gorse had encroached on the hillsides. It looked like it had smothered out the trees. This was worrisome, as she saw a couple of new houses on the hillside, surrounded by the spiny plants. As the light faded, the cold seeped through their coats. Shivering, they headed back to the warmth of their car and returned the way they had come.

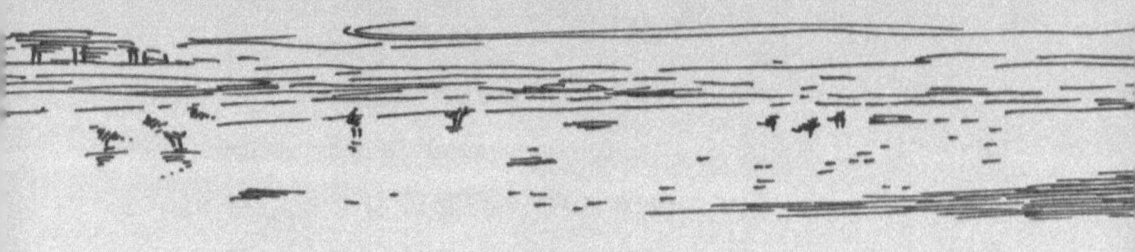

CHAPTER FOURTEEN

THE GIRL WHO TALKED TO BIRDS

THE SISTERS DROVE SLOWLY back to town. They passed the old McGinley place. It was still there, surrounded by fir and cedar trees. Alicia pondered out loud, "I wonder who lives in the McGinley place. Remember Colleen? She made local headlines back in the late 50s.

"I have a vague recollection that something terrible happened to her. Do you know the story?"

"I'll never forget it. It happened during my sophomore year in high school. It was a strange case. Apparently, she thought she was getting messages from sea gulls."

COLLEEN McGINLEY

Colleen was odd. Everybody knew it, even her own family admitted it. Born in 1940, the youngest child in a family of five boys and three girls, she was in turn adored and ignored. Her older sisters doted on her in their own careless way. Her bemused mother loved her vaguely. She was tired and left much of the care up to the big sisters. Barbara was ten and Louisa was six when Colleen came along. They loved to dress her up and rock her to sleep. Barbara became adept at changing diapers and giving her a bottle. They played house with her. They were sure she was the prettiest baby in the world, with her big hazel eyes and thick auburn hair.

The boys were amused by her but not as prone to play with her as they were wary of diapers that needed changing.

As she grew, she became a scrapper, fighting for toys with Louisa and four-year-old Arnold. She learned early on to dodge her unruly siblings as they tore around the too-small house, chasing one another and wrestling. Their mother would not allow any rough housing in the kitchen, but the rest of the house was fair game. In the long winter months, the wind and rains kept them mostly indoors. It helped that the older boys found an outlet for their energy by being involved in sports at school.

They lived four miles from town, on a small acreage surrounded by woods. The back of the property ended at the beach. There was a large shed, where they kept tools, the woodpile and assorted machinery. A little farther from the house was a chicken coop, which was their egg supply and source of Sunday dinner. Their car and pickup were left outdoors in the rain.

Their bursting-at-the-seams house had three bedrooms and one bathroom, with an extra bedroom added onto the big front porch for the two oldest boys, Charles, sixteen, and Patrick, fifteen. The girls all shared a room with bunk beds, and the younger boys shared a bunk room also.

The kitchen was off the dining room, which opened onto the living room. There was a big, old-fashioned radio in the living room, their entertainment center. They all gathered around it in the evenings after the dishes were done to listen to their favorite programs—Jack Benny, Red Skelton, or "The Shadow," or, perhaps, "Our Miss Brooks." The boys' favorite was "The Lone Ranger." After their programs they scattered off to do their homework, various chores or bed.

Their mother, Mary, worked hard, cooking on the big wood range, doing the laundry, sewing, canning in season, tending her garden, caring for her brood. She was a rather simple, plain woman with a good heart, and a devout Catholic. She would fight to the death for her children. When one of them (always one of the boys) got into trouble at school, she was right there, doing battle for the miscreant. The boys tended to be a bit wild, and sometimes got into fights at school, or sassed a teacher. She would talk to the teacher and persuade him or her to give the guilty boy another chance. They would take pity on her and sentence the boys to a few hours of detention after school.

She did her best to teach the boys some manners and curb their willfulness but was not very successful. The three youngest ones were especially unruly. She found that her wooden spoon was her best tool for persuading them to behave. All she had to do was reach for it and give them a threatening glare and they would clear out of her area. She rarely told their father about their misbehavior because he had a short fuse and would sometimes wallop the boys with his belt. Even so, every night she would make them all kneel and say a rosary with her.

Michael, the father, was a rough and tumble logger. He would occasionally take the boys hunting or fishing, but otherwise left the bulk of the parenting up to Mary. He frequently stopped by the local pub on his way home from work and sometimes didn't get home until after the children were all in bed. Occasionally, he would roar into the house drunk, and slam things around in the kitchen until Mary got out of bed and made him something to eat. He was never an abusive drunk, just loud and extremely jolly. Sometimes he would stagger into the bedroom and throw himself down on top of the bed, fully clothed. Then Mary would get up and remove his muddy boots and throw a blanket over him. She would sometimes get so angry with him that she wouldn't speak to him for days, but he could always, eventually, sweet talk her out of her anger. She told herself that he deserved the odd drink now and then because he worked so hard, and he wasn't abusive like her father. He did love his kids and kept a roof over their heads.

Colleen showed an affinity for the animals at a very early age. She loved the chickens. She spent a lot of time watching them and talking to them. One day, when she was four, she overheard her mother tell Patrick to go get Colleen's favorite red hen and chop off its head for dinner. "It's getting old and not laying much anymore. Time for chicken and dumplings."

Patrick went out to get the hen but could not find it. It was missing from the henhouse. Puzzled, he expanded his search into the area around the henhouse and into the surrounding brush. He finally found Colleen, huddled under the bushes, cuddling the hen. When he tried to pry it out of her hands, she scuttled off into the woods with it. No amount of hollering would bring her back.

When he reported what had happened to Mary, she let out an exasperated sigh. "That girl. If she had her way, we'd never have a chicken dinner. All right, Patrick, let's have one of the other hens. That big speckled one. It's not earning its keep either."

So, the red hen was saved, and Colleen guarded it until it died of old age.

As Colleen grew, she began to wander off into the woods around their house when the weather was decent. She loved exploring the secretive hiding places under the overhanging brush. She would sit on the soft moss and watch the bugs going about their business, and the spiders making their webs. It was so nice and quiet away from the noisy house. Sometimes she would study the fluid, effortless movements of the squirrels as they flung themselves through the tree branches. She was sure that fairies lived in the cool recesses of the forest glades and kept a sharp eye out for them.

Her siblings roamed the woods too, when their chores were done. Sometimes they built "forts," out of tree branches and brush, and would let her come with them. The girls liked to bring snacks and books into their secret hideouts and would spend hours playing house or reading or making up stories for each other.

Colleen really preferred to be alone. She loved to watch the birds and study their habits. Her noisy siblings would scare them off. Alone, she would insert her body into a small space under the trees, breathing in their sweet scent, and watch and listen. She heard the trees talking to each other in the breeze. She strained to decipher what they were saying. She was sure they had many stories to tell. But she never quite learned their language.

Colleen sought out the wildflowers that were abundant in the area. She loved the trilliums, first flowers of the spring that glowed white in the deep shade, and the purple and yellow wild violets and bleeding hearts. The wild rhododendrons put on a lovely, pink display in the spring, as did the wild azaleas. She loved to sniff their spicy fragrance. Sometimes she would pick a bouquet to take home to her mother. But usually, she left them alone to continue blooming.

As Colleen went into grade school, she became more and more introverted. She sat quietly in class, much to the delight of the teachers who had taught the noisy siblings who had gone before her. And she seemed to absorb whatever they taught with little effort. But she was hesitant to speak up in class. At recess, she would slip down into the creek bottom behind the school and look for frogs and salamanders and interesting bugs and butterflies. She found the shy violets that bloomed there and daisies. She was sure the fairies used the stream for their fairy boats. Sometimes she would miss the bell and be late getting back to class because she was absorbed in watching the pollywogs wriggling around in the creek. This would get her extra homework, and notes sent home.

Mary would read the notes—"Colleen is a good student but she needs to pay better attention in class and come in from recess on time. She may have to be kept after school if she can't pay attention to the bell." She would lecture Colleen and then wait for the next note.

When Colleen was six, she realized that the sea gulls were communicating with her. She was exploring the driftwood on the beach with her sisters and Arnold and Charles. The gulls caught her eye and she stopped to watch them. She loved the big, pure white birds with their bright yellow beaks with a small, bright red jewel like spot on the bottom front, sharp, beady eyes and clean black trim feathers. One large one perched on a log near her and watched her intently. She sat still and watched back. She held up her hand. "Hi, beautiful bird. Did you want to talk to me?"

The bird tilted his head, questioning. He lifted his wings and waved them and settled back firmly on his feet. His head bobbed up and down. He took a step towards her. She held her breath. She reached out slowly and gently touched his wing.

Arnold noticed what she was doing and stood, watching her. He nudged Louisa and nodded towards the scene. Gradually, the children all stopped what they were doing and stared. Colleen was petting a sea gull. And talking to it. The older children moved in closer, causing the bird to take off into the air and join the other gulls cruising in the sky.

"How did you do that, Colleen?" asked Arnold.

She looked at him with wondering eyes. "I don't know. I was just sitting here, and he came up and talked to me."

The others laughed. Arnold was curious. "What did he say?"

Colleen's face closed up. She frowned. "That's for me to know and you to find out."

Back at the house, the children reported the incident to their mother, who smiled her tired smile and said, "That's nice. I wish I could talk to the birds. Good for you, Colleen." And she gave her a hug. Colleen smiled happily.

A couple of months later, the four youngest children were again playing among the piles of driftwood. Colleen looked up and saw the gulls wheeling in the air above her. Suddenly, they started diving at her, beating at her with their wings, driving her up the bank towards the higher ground along the beachfront. Her siblings saw the birds chasing her and all ran to help her. She was driven all the way up to the top of the bank, screaming all the way, with the rest of the children in hot pursuit. As they crested the top of the rocky ridge, the birds whirled away and swept up into the air and out over the surf. At the same time, a gigantic, rogue wave rolled onto the beach and swept all the way to the top of the embankment, tossing huge chunks of driftwood and bleached logs here and there like twigs. The children stared at the chaos. Slowly, they all turned and looked at Colleen.

Finally, Arnold, in an awed voice, said, "The gulls saved us. They were chasing you and they saved all of us. We could have all been killed."

Colleen was shaking and somber. "I...I think they like me."

The children burst into the house that afternoon. They were all shouting at once except for Colleen. Babbling youngsters, all telling the story at once, surrounded their mother. Mary had a hard time getting them to quiet down. Finally, she said firmly, "Arnold, tell me what's happened and the rest of you be quiet."

"The gulls saved us, Arnold gasped. "We were playing in the driftwood and the gulls started attacking Colleen and chasing her up the bank and we all tried to help her and a giant wave came in and covered the whole beach and we would have drowned."

Mary gasped and stared at them, wide eyed. "That's horrible! Was anybody hurt? Do you mean that the sea gulls forced you to all get out of the way of the wave?"

"Yes," they shouted. And immediately erupted into babbling racket again.

Mary, exasperated, finally shouted, "Quiet!" As they calmed down, she turned to Colleen. "Colleen, are you all right? Did the gulls hurt you?"

"Oh no, Mommy. They wouldn't hurt me. They saved me. They saved all of us." Her face was solemn, her eyes glistening with tears. "The ocean tried to grab me, but the gulls wouldn't let it."

Mary sat down abruptly and gazed at them all. Finally, she let out a big sigh. She grabbed Colleen and hugged her hard. "I'm so glad you're all right. From now on I'm going to appreciate those gulls." She paused. They needed a distraction. "Now, how about hot chocolate all around?"

The children shouted their enthusiasm for that idea and, in the ensuing scuffle around the kitchen table gradually calmed down and enjoyed their treat.

That night Mary told Michael about the incident. He shook his head in amazement. "I think Colleen has something special. She seems to be able to talk to the other creatures around here and they seem to follow her every move. The dogs and cats even follow her around. She's an odd little duck. Thank God the kids are all right."

Gradually the story faded into family lore, passed on to friends and relatives. But as time went by, Colleen became known as that odd girl who talks to birds."

As the years went by, Colleen was considered one of the weird ones at school. Most of the other kids either ignored her or made fun of her. While she kept to herself, she quietly turned in her homework regularly, always neatly done. Her teachers liked and encouraged her. She was a good student but ignored student activities. She preferred to read and write wherever she could find a quiet place. She ignored current fashion trends among the student body and wore whatever was clean in her closet when she got dressed. She wore dark-rimmed glasses and plain oxfords. She managed to become friends with two other girls who were studious types, Melanie and Leona. They ate lunch together and supported each other. They discussed boys and the future and their studies. Sometimes Colleen would lead her friends on expeditions in the forest or on the beach. Rarely, she would go to a school dance or a movie with one of the nerdy boys who were attracted to her. They were friends but never bothered with romantic entanglements, in spite of an occasional kiss goodnight.

When the girls graduated, Barbara and Louisa went to college, so they rarely saw each other and, gradually, lost touch. Colleen went to work at the Starfish Cafe, out on the south jetty. She was a fine student but was not interested in leaving town to go to college. She had no money anyway, other than a few hundred dollars she had in the bank from babysitting and odd jobs. She loved the view from the cafe and worked quietly and efficiently. The customers liked her and so did her employer.

She walked the beach whenever the weather permitted. The locals weren't surprised when the gulls followed her. Sometimes she would throw them bits of fish scraps that she picked up at the docks. The fishermen all knew her and saved scraps when they were cleaning their fish,

She lived at home with her parents, who worried about her future. Her siblings were all out of the house, married or pursuing careers in other towns that offered better opportunities. She spent her spare time journaling, sketching and observing the world around her. Once in a while she would go to a movie or a church gathering with her co-workers from the restaurant. She dreamed that someday she would marry and have a family. Meanwhile, she was content to wait for her life to unfold.

One day she was walking on the beach after her shift at the restaurant. It was summer, so the sun was still hanging in the western sky at eight o'clock. She wore a red windbreaker to ward off the cold evening breeze. She paused to breathe in the fresh ocean air. She turned and saw a man standing near the water's edge, fishing in the surf. As she approached, she noticed gulls wheeling in the sky above him. Soon she was close enough to speak, and they flew away. She knew this meeting was important.

"Hello?" she called.

He turned. He was nearly a head taller than she, with black hair and dark brown, piercing eyes. She recognized him immediately. Taylor Malloy, two grades ahead of her in school. Her heart skipped a beat. She had nourished a crush on this boy since they were in grade school. They had rarely spoken. He seemed to live in a world foreign to hers. He was popular in school and very athletic. She followed his high school career from the orbit of her own planet, wishing he would notice her. But he never seemed to do so.

The only thing she could think to say was, "How's the fishing?"

"The fishin's great, but the catchin' not so much." He grinned and looked at her closely. "Don't I know you? You were behind me in school."

Colleen's face felt hot. "Yes, you graduated two years ahead of me. What are you doing these days?"

"Well, I tried college for a few semesters and then decided it wasn't what I wanted to do. I'm working on my dad's charter fishing boat these days. I plan to own my own soon. I decided I'm a fisherman at heart and that's what I want to do. How about you? I know you were at the top of your class. Are you in college?"

She was surprised that he knew anything about her. "No, I guess I'm just a hometown girl. I prefer to stay here.

I'm working at the Starfish Cafe until something better opens up. It's a fun place to work and I can see the ocean out the windows while I'm working." She was amazed that she could talk so easily with this man she had admired for so long. How was it that they hadn't run into each other on the docks before now?

He smiled. "I guess you're crazy about the sea, just like me. I'd rather be out there anytime than anywhere else." He paused and looked at her closely. "I remember now, they say you're the girl who talks to sea gulls. Do you still do that?"

Colleen looked at her feet. "I'm not crazy, if that's what you're implying. I just love the gulls, and they seem to like me back. Sometimes when they're hovering around me, I sense that they're trying to tell me something." She looked up at him. "I just get these feelings from them, like they're trying to communicate. But I'm not crazy."

"Gosh, I didn't mean to suggest that you're mental. I just think maybe you have a rare gift for communing with'em. I wish I could talk to'em. They could tell me where the fish are and keep an eye on the weather for me. It'd be a really useful skill for a fisherman."

She squinted at him and decided he wasn't mocking her. "Actually, you're right. I can always sense when a storm's brewing at sea."

"You know, I'm done fishing for the day. Would you like to come and have a cup of coffee with me? Or maybe an ice cream?"

Colleen's heart raced. She smiled. "I'd love to."

Taylor reeled in his line and picked up his gear. "My pickup's parked over by the restroom. My hands are kind of slimy from handling the bait. Do you mind waiting in my truck while I wash up?"

"No problem." They walked back to his pickup and Colleen waited for him there. She did a quick check-up on her appearance, combing her hair and touching up her lipstick, her only nod to makeup. Large hazel, dark-fringed eyes looked back at her from her compact mirror. She studied her face. Her nose was a little bit crooked, which always irked her, but she had a nice, wide mouth and a well-rounded chin. She had a full head of naturally curly hair, which she could never tame. She wasn't beautiful, but she wasn't ugly either. Some people might say she was attractive. She felt excited and fatalistic at the same time. The birds had meant him for her, she just knew it.

They were married six months later in the little Catholic Church on the hill that her family had always attended. Colleen felt like she was watching from outside her body as she glided down the aisle towards the man she knew was meant for her. But her face glowed. She was twenty, in love, and knew this was where she should be.

Her extended family was there, and his smaller family group, and a few friends. Her happy family made the reception afterwards loud and lively, with young nieces and nephews running underfoot. Her parents laughed a lot. Alice knew they were relieved to see her so happy and settled at last.

In the middle of the afternoon, they slipped away. They drove up the coast for their four-day honeymoon, enjoying the view as they went. They stayed in a place that overlooked the beach and made love where they could see and hear the sea.

They settled in a little rental house, covered with weathered gray cedar siding, not far from the bluff where all the kids parked to make out. Colleen loved their cozy home. They painted the rooms a soft yellow to make them warm and cheerful. They made love on their new bed in their freshly painted bedroom. They spent every minute they could spare in their busy lives together.

Taylor worked the swing shift at the mill, which allowed him to work for his father in the daytime on the charter boat. Colleen worked extra shifts at the restaurant to help build up their savings.

Their favorite sound was the ocean's roar. Colleen would warn Taylor when she thought a storm was coming up out at sea, and he usually heeded her warnings.

The day came when he had his own charter boat, which he named "Colleen," and was making regular trips out through the narrow waterway between the stone jetties. The river meets the sea here, and sometimes it looks like the bodies of water are fighting each other, when the tide is coming in. The waves can be huge and fierce. Colleen often watched Taylor's boat go out with her heart in her throat until he was safely at sea. Sometimes, when the boat came back in over the bar, it would almost disappear in the troughs between the waves. Eventually, they planned for her to quit her job and help Taylor on the boat. Colleen was excited about the prospect.

One morning, Colleen looked out her kitchen window and saw that the gulls had gathered in her backyard. They were standing or sitting there, all facing toward her window. They were watching her.

Suddenly she was filled with a sense of dread. Trembling, she stopped packing Taylor's lunch and ran into the bedroom where he was getting dressed.

"Taylor, you can't take the boat out today. Someone is going to be killed. There's a disturbance at sea. I don't know what it is, but it's terrible."

He looked at her, frowning. "But, Honey, I have to go out today. I've got six guys who've paid for this trip. The weather station's predicting good weather."

She grabbed him around the chest and hugged him. "Please, please don't go out today. You can take them tomorrow. Or give them their money back."

He stroked her back. "I can't postpone this trip," he said slowly. "They're coming all the way from Eugene and it's too late to tell them to come tomorrow. Besides, we need the money. If I tell them my wife doesn't want me to go out, they'll never hire me again. I'll keep a sharp eye out for anything that's unusual. I'm sure we'll be fine."

He held her at arm's length. "You know I'm the super skipper. I know how to handle my boat, and I know how to read the ocean. We'll be fine."

She continued to plead with him until he snapped at her. "It'll be okay. Stop worrying!" He tore away, grabbed his lunch pail and slammed out the door.

She was sobbing as she drove down to the jetty to watch him go out over the bar. Waiting there, almost paralyzed with fear, she watched his boat come down the river. As they passed by, Taylor saw her standing there and waved. She refused to wave back and watched as he made it over the bar and out to sea. That was the last time she saw him.

She dragged herself to work, hoping for a busy day to keep herself occupied.

Around noon, the Coast Guard received a distress call from the boat. They immediately went out looking for the "Colleen." Somehow, the sea had swallowed the boat and everyone on board. They were puzzled. The seas were rough but not unmanageable. Taylor had a fine reputation as a skipper, and they knew he didn't take careless chances. What had happened? It was a mystery.

After hours of searching, they managed to find an oil slick, and a couple of life vests floating on the water. But that was all. Taylor and his boat and clients had all vanished.

Eventually, two of his clients' bodies were found washed up on the beach near Port Orford. The rest of the men were simply gone. There was a lot of wild speculation about what had happened. Perhaps a whale had rammed them, or a rogue wave had swamped them. Maybe they had engine trouble, and the boat was tipped over by a freak wave and sank. Maybe they had run into drug runners. There was no way to know.

Colleen was inconsolable. No one could comfort her. She would go and stand on the south jetty and watch out to sea, hoping his body would somehow float home. Her parents visited her often in the evenings and after church on Sunday. They tried to convince her to move back home. Her siblings called or stopped by frequently.

After four months of watching, she decided she couldn't do this anymore. And she couldn't live without him. She drove down to the south jetty and parked her car facing the sea. She sat and watched the waves for a long time. A large flock of gulls began whirling around over her car. Finally, she got out, walked to the top of the jetty, and began making her way over the huge boulders towards the distant end of it. The gulls kept circling around her. As she neared the end of the jetty, picking her way over the slippery stone surfaces, they began to scream. People were gathering on the beach, drawn to the spectacle, not sure what to do. The gulls swooped and swirled around Colleen, trying to drive her back. The crowd watching thought they were attacking her, but she beat them off and stubbornly continued out to the end.

The tide was coming in and the end of the jetty was blasted by the huge rollers. The icy spray slammed against her body, stinging her face. She faced the sea, held up her fists and screamed, "Here I am. You wanted me, now take me."

A few moments she stood there as the local police, who had been called, tried to work their way out to her. They hadn't gone far when, like a scene from a horror film, a monster wave reared up over her head, and took her from the boulder. For a few terrible moments, the observers could see her head bob out of the waves as the gulls followed her. She was swept out to sea, and then vanished from sight. The gulls continued to circle in the air, screaming, for a long time.

They never found her body. But the local folk believe that the girl who talked to the gulls had joined her beloved out in the deep. The town mourned another sea tragedy, as Colleen became part of the lore that was passed on from generation to generation. And parents used the story to warn their children not to turn their backs on the ocean, or the gulls.

Alicia shook her head. "It was such a tragic thing. They were a great couple, and people liked them. People talked about it for a long time."

Sophie sighed. "That's so sad." She shivered. "This may be a small town but there are so many stories." She paused. "Are you hungry? I am. Let's go find a place to eat on the waterfront."

Alicia stepped on the gas.

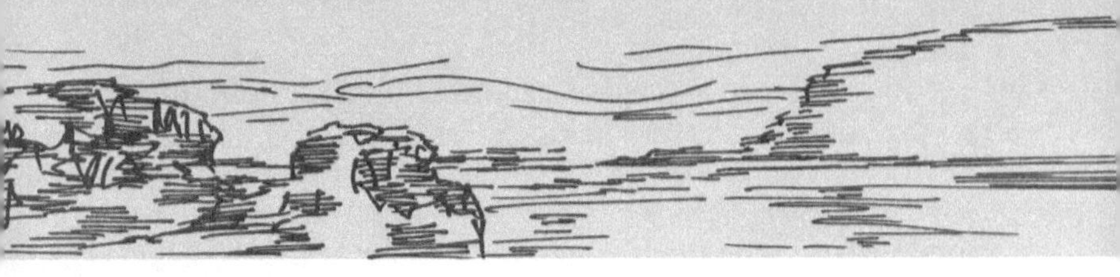

CHAPTER FIFTEEN

TIT FOR TAT

ALLIE AND SOPHIE drove back into town. On the way, they passed the posh golf course that was drawing in golfers from all over the world. Allie glanced at the sign for it. "I know a few golfers who would like to play there. Never took up the sport myself. But it's been a boon to the town."

"Yeah. Steve would love to play there but we could never afford it."

"I hear it's quite expensive. We've eaten at the dining room in the past. They have good food. I'm glad that Tom isn't a golfer, though. It's an expensive hobby."

Sophie shrugged. "Yeah, but Steve enjoys it. And it's his only sport. So, I encourage him to go for it at the local links."

The sisters looked for a place to eat along the riverfront. They decided upon a small place on the docks, where they were sure to get fresh seafood. Both ordered fish and chips, and enjoyed the fresh, flaky fish with the crisp fries and slaw. The steaming coffee perked them up and they decided to make one last trip down to the beach before turning in.

They watched the sunset as it turned the clouds crimson and gold and waited for the trail of flashing gold to recede from shore and over the horizon. Then returned to their room, watched the news, and got ready for bed.

Allie went to close the window shades and stood looking down on the main street. It was quiet for a Friday night. A bright light bled out into the foggy street from the only bar in her line of sight, but the sound was subdued. It was different back in the days of "Big Al" McCloud. Then, there were more bars on the strip and Friday night could get wild and raucous. The loggers and millworkers were known for roaring in on the weekends and occasionally getting into drunken brawls.

Allie remembered "Big Al" from her school days. A giant of a man, he was six foot six and all muscle. A Korean war vet, dark haired and handsome, he was respected by all, even the unruly loggers. All he had to do was walk into a bar where a fight was brewing, and the men would calm down. Peace was restored. He rarely had to knock heads together. Nobody wanted to cross him. It wasn't because he was mean or a bully. He was good-natured and gentle, slow to anger, but firm. Most people liked him. But everybody knew that he wouldn't stand for any nonsense. The kids in town were in awe of him.

BIG AL McCLOUD

Al was the police chief for at least thirty years in Bandon. He had a series of deputies who shared duties with him. One of his deputies was Mel Johnson. Everybody in town disliked him because he never passed up on an opportunity to hand out a traffic ticket. He was sneaky about it, hiding behind stores or signs, just waiting for someone to zip by too fast. He even gave Big Al's wife, Rose, a ticket.

Big Al was a thirty-three-year-old Korean War vet when he married his much-adored Rose. Rose, an "old maid" of twenty-six, was the town librarian. At five foot six, she looked tiny and fragile next to her big husband. But pretty Rose had her giant eating out of her hand. She could do no wrong, as far as her husband was concerned. But he stood firm when she tried to get him to fix her ticket. She was furious.

She put her fists on her hips and glared at him. "Why won't you do this for me?" she snapped. "After all I've done for you and this town. This town owes me. I wouldn't have been speeding if I hadn't been late for work because I was working on that bazaar project to help Maddy out. Besides, there wasn't any traffic to speak of and I wasn't speeding that much. And he was so sneaky about it, hiding behind the service station."

Al gave her a sad-eyed look and stood his ground. "I'm sorry, Honey, but I can't do it. It would look bad to the whole town. You know how everybody talks. If I fixed your ticket, then everybody would expect me to do it. Besides, you and I have to set an example for the young folks. You'll just have to pay the fine and be done with it. Besides, it's embarrassing to have my own wife caught speeding. Let's just pay it and forget about it."

"You make me so mad. Nobody has to know about it. You can tell Mel to keep his mouth shut if he wants to keep his job. Fifty dollars is a lot of money."

"Rose, I won't do that. I can't believe you'd even suggest it. I don't want to hear any more about it."

Rose clamped her mouth shut and stomped into the kitchen. Fuming, she slammed pots and pans around as she threw together their dinner. She didn't speak to him all through the (singed) meal or for the rest of the evening. It was several days before they kissed and made up. But she never forgot what Mel had done to her and kept her eye out for a chance to get even with him.

An eager-beaver, Mel loved catching culprits. There wasn't much traffic in Bandon, which caused most people to get heavy footed on the gas pedal when they thought he wasn't around. Mel was very good at lurking around town and wrote out tickets with alarming regularity. He handed out tickets for taillights that weren't working, and for not signaling for turns, or not coming to a complete stop at stop signs. He hauled in juveniles who snitched soda pop from the corner store, or broke a neighbor's window, or got into their parent's beer and drank too much. He hauled in drunks who disturbed the peace. He kept the jail busy. He was proud of his righteousness and keeping the town orderly. The teenage boys who could drive detested him and laughed at him behind his back.

One day, Mel noticed the new waitress at the City Limits Grill, a greasy spoon on the highway south of town, where many of the local businessmen gathered for lunch. He flirted with Maxine and ogled her as she waited on the other customers. She kept herself clean and didn't flirt back with the men. She was prim and proper and wore her mousy brown hair in a tidy bun on top of her head. Mel watched her for months before he finally worked up the nerve to ask her out.

Maxine looked at Mel, took in his thinning crew cut, his skinny five-foot-eight frame, and his uniform and gulped.

It had occurred to her that she was going nowhere in this burg and had few options. She lived with her overbearing parents in a house where she had to share a room with her sister. She thought, Why not? At least he's clean and law-abiding. She said, "Okay. But I have to be in by midnight."

Mel and Maxine went out for several weeks before he had the nerve to kiss her. After that, things heated up. They decided to get married. Mel was ecstatic. Maxine was resigned. Her parents were euphoric, and immediately began planning a big wedding they couldn't afford to usher their daughter out of the house. Big Al was pleased. He needed a good, if over-zealous, deputy. If Mel got married, he would be less likely to pull up stakes and go elsewhere.

On the day before the wedding, Mel came into the police station carrying a pair of newly polished dress shoes. He'd had them resoled and polished to a military shine at the shoe repair shop. He would look spiffy for the wedding ceremony. He proudly showed them to Al, who whistled. "Wow, I can see myself in those. Pretty sharp."

Mel beamed. "I'll come back for 'em when my shift is done." He set them on a shelf behind the counter for safekeeping.

Rose happened to be visiting Big Al at the time and watched as Mel left to finish his shift. She was sitting by Al's desk when Arlene Frick came shuffling in. She greeted Rose and looked at Al. "Al, I've locked myself out of my car. Can you help me?"

"Sure, Arlene. Let me get my tool." Al pulled out a wire clothes hanger he kept for just this purpose. "Will you catch the phone, Honey?"

Rose grinned. "Sure, Al. Be glad to. And good luck, Arlene."

As soon as Al and Arlene walked out the door, Rose picked up Mel's shoes and slipped into the storeroom. She knew there was a paintbrush, and a can of white paint kept there for touch-ups on the walls that were frequently scraped by the comings and goings of the citizenry through the police station. Al liked to keep things tidy.

She opened the paint can, grabbed a stick and gave it a good stir. Then she picked up the smallest brush she could find and began to paint on the soles of the shoes. She finished quickly, slipped into the women's restroom, and placed the shoes on the open windowsill with the soles facing out to dry.

She returned to the desk and sat waiting for Al. After half an hour he came back in. "She was parked clear at the other end of the street. It took longer than I expected. Were there any calls?"

"All's quiet on the western front," she replied.

Al sat down and they visited for a few minutes. Then Rose stretched and stood up. "I'm going to the restroom and then on home. I have to iron my dress for the big wedding tomorrow."

"Okay, I'll see you when I get home." Al gave her a peck on the cheek and pulled some paperwork in front of him.

Rose went into the lady's room and checked the bottoms of the shoes. They felt dry enough. At least the Bandon wind was good for something. She closed the window and stealthily slipped out and placed them back on the shelf.

The next day she watched as Mel walked out in front of the altar of St. John's Episcopal Church. Al, the best man, accompanied him.

Maxine, her face pale, wearing a billowing white dress, smiled a tremulous smile as she enjoyed her moment in the limelight. She walked down the aisle on her smiling father's arm as the organist loudly played a wedding march.

Mel, in a trance, took her arm and together they turned toward the altar. They stepped up on the dais and knelt down together. Suddenly there was a wave of titters from the front to the back of the church. Al's eyebrows shot up and he glanced at Rose. He stoically maintained a sober expression. Mel glanced back with a questioning look. He couldn't see what was going on, so faced the front steadily until the ceremony was over. The priest presented the new husband and wife to the congregation, and they walked quickly down the aisle to the cheers and clapping of the grinning guests.

When Rose rejoined Al at the reception, he looked at her suspiciously. "You wouldn't have any idea how the word 'HELP' got written on the soles of his shoes, would you?"

Rose giggled. "That'll teach him to give me a ticket. Wait till you see what we did to his car."

"Is there anything else I should know?"

She smiled up at him. "Let's just enjoy the reception. Then we'll talk about the 'shivaree' I have planned." They headed for their table.

He was enthralled that she
could sing so beautifully and
play the piano so well.

CHAPTER SIXTEEN

REMEMBERING ELLA

THAT EVENING, Allie and Sophie, cozy in their beds, watched an old movie on TV, The End of the Affair. As the closing credits rolled, Allie clicked off the TV. She lay back down, watching the shadows on the ceiling. Suddenly, she piped up. "Hey, Soph, remember Ella Mae Goldberger? You know, the crippled lady who lived up the street from here?

Sophie yawned. "Wasn't she a friend of Mom's?

"Yeah. I guess the movie brought her to mind. Did Mom ever tell you the story about her and the school principal?

Sophie rolled over in bed, propped herself up on her elbow. "Okay! Now you have to tell me, or I won't be able to get to sleep. You're not saying she had an affair with him."

Allie laughed. "No, no. But she pulled off something she never told anyone but Mom about. It was wild. Anyway, you won't believe this. Ella Mae had a heart of gold, but she taught the principal a hard lesson."

ELLA MAE

Allie sat up and faced Sophie. "When I was in high school, Ella Mae was well known in the town. She was crippled when she was young and wore a brace on her leg and used canes to get around. When she was in her early twenties, before she was crippled, she had her own radio show on the local radio station. This was before television reached the area. She accompanied herself on the piano and sang the songs of the day, interspersed with local news and gossip, occasional recipes, and announcements. She sometimes read her fan letters on the air. She had a beautiful voice and was quite popular in the area. She was thrilled when a Portland radio station invited her to come in for an interview. This was the big time. She made the trip and sat through an interview, which she said she thought went well. Then she went home to wait for them to contact her.

'Three days later, she awoke in the middle of the night with a raging fever and began vomiting uncontrollably. Her body ached everywhere, and her legs felt stiff. At first, she thought it was just the flu. She was living with her parents at the time, and they were very concerned. When her condition didn't improve over the next day, they insisted on taking her to the emergency room at the hospital. At the hospital, they ran tests and immediately put her in isolation. She had polio.

'She spent two weeks in the hospital, then went to rehabilitation. Her fans flooded her with cards and good wishes, but that didn't ease her bitter disappointment. Her career was over.

'When Ella Mae finally got back home, braces and all, she was deeply depressed. Her only consolation was playing the piano; the only activity that interested her

'As months went by, she continued working on getting her strength and her mobility back. Her right leg was nearly normal, but her left leg needed a brace. She used a cane to get around. But she was still fragile and depressed.

'Her mother was worried about her and kept looking for something for her to do that wasn't too strenuous. One day, she saw an ad in the local paper for a cooking class being taught by a local chef at the culinary institute in the community college. She persuaded Ella to go and try it, just for fun. That's where Ella met Rodger Johnson.

'Rodger was passionate about food. He loved to show the local women (and occasional brave man) how to cook amazing meals using the locally grown and harvested foods. Ella Mae looked at the six-foot, red haired, freckled food enthusiast and fell in love. Rodger took one look at Ella, intrigued. He liked her dark-fringed brown eyes and shiny black hair, tied back with a red ribbon. She seemed fragile and yet determined. She followed his instructions with great enthusiasm, if not great success, and he was amused. By the end of the series of six classes, he was hooked.

'Rodger courted Ella with fine food and wine, and after a few months they were married. Ella found a job as a receptionist at a local real estate office, and Rodger continued working in one of the better restaurants in town, and teaching at the Culinary Institute. But Rodger had bigger ambitions. He wanted to open his own restaurant. They squirreled away every extra cent they could in a savings account until they could make a down payment on his own place.

'Ella kept working on improving her walking ability and made some progress. But she never could throw away her cane or brace. She decided that she could face the future as long as she had Rodger by her side. He did everything he could to help her with her walking and supported her in all that she wanted to do. He was enthralled that she could sing so beautifully and play the piano so well. She managed to pick up a part-time job playing for a local pub three times a week. It helped her sustain her interest in her career.

One day, she passed out at the office. They tested her at the emergency room and kept her overnight. The doctors concluded that her heart was weak, and that she had rebound symptoms of polio, and told her that she should quit her job, and avoid stress. She could end up an invalid. They gave her a prescription for high blood pressure and sent her home.

This frightened her and Rodger, and he insisted that she quit her office job. However, he did encourage her to use her talent at the pub, because she needed that creative outlet. So, she played on, enjoyed it, and accumulated her tips and small wages.

Ella's parents loved Rodger and wanted to help him with his dream. They offered to loan him $4,000 from their savings. With that, plus the savings the couple had scraped up, they bought an older, Cape Cod style house, near the waterfront in Bandon. Rodger had done his homework, and figured that Bandon needed a good restaurant to attract tourists as well as locals. He spent eight months renovating it to suit his needs, which included a brand-new chef's kitchen. He kept the character of the charming old place, which looked like it had been plucked right out of New England, with its gray shingles and blue door. Ella did what she could to help, shopping for furnishings, painting as much as her body would let her. She saw to it that a piano was installed in the dining room so she could play for the customers.

'Despite her delicate health, the bond between Rodger and Ella only grew stronger. They rented a nice cottage on the upper edge of town, in a quiet neighborhood and settled in. At first, Ella provided background music at the restaurant, using the piano she had purchased. She played softly and occasionally sang to her own accompaniment. The customers liked her and filled her tip jar on the nights she played. The restaurant gradually picked up a steady clientele. Rodger was in his element.

'Eventually, Ella decided that she would like to bring in extra income and started teaching piano lessons in the afternoons. That's when Mom met Ella. I tried to learn piano for a year and then decided that it wasn't for me. But Mom and Ella hit it off and became very good friends.

'I really liked Ella. She was sweet and funny and tried her best to teach me. But I was a poor student. Besides, Mom and Dad couldn't really afford it, and it just wasn't my thing. So, I quit.

'Rodger was happily involved with his business and Ella was happy that he was happy. Over the next ten years they developed a comfortable routine. He kept Sundays and Mondays free to spend with her. The rest of the week, he spent long hours in his restaurant. But before he went to work each day, he prepared a nice breakfast for Ella, and helped her get up and get dressed. She was getting weaker and unable to stand for long periods of time. It was difficult for her to get into her clothing.

'Ella liked to practice her music a couple of hours every day. Her piano was situated on the opposite wall from her big picture window on the street side of the house. There was a big mirror above the piano so she could keep an eye on what went on outside. One day she was working on a new piece and happened to glance up just in time to see the high school principal, Mr. Carlson, walking down the street, carrying a cup of coffee. Everyone knew who he was, as he was frequently featured in the local paper. She was surprised that he'd be out there on a school day. She assumed that he was on his lunch hour and had a mission. She was shocked to see him pause in front of the house opposite her own, glance up and down the street, then surreptitiously sidle around the house to slip in the side door.

'Now, Ella knew that neighbor well. She was young and pretty and involved in many activities in town, including the PTA. Why would Mr. Carlson be sneaking into her house in the middle of the day? School business? Fat chance.

'As weeks went by, Ella observed the strange behavior but didn't say anything. It happened a couple of times a week. She figured it was none of her business. But couldn't help being curious.

'Bored with her confined life, Ella decided to start a little business of her own to bring in more income. Rodger was making enough to keep the restaurant open and a roof over their heads, and pay back her parents for the loan, but she wanted to contribute so that they could afford a few luxuries. Besides, she needed to be out among people more. She notified her two piano students that she would not be available in the future and, after diligent research, bought into a high-end costume jewelry business. After arranging with the local supermarket to rent a corner of the store by the entrance, she set up her stand. It was perfect for her. She could visit with the locals who came in without exerting herself as she sat behind her counter. She did surprisingly well for several months.

'One day, Mom came into the store and stopped to chat. Ella was crying. When asked what was wrong, she sniffled. "Oh Laura, I've done a terrible thing. I wanted to make a big profit during the Christmas season to show Rodger that my little adventure was paying off. So, I took all our savings out of the bank, $1,200, and bought a big load of stock. And now it isn't selling and I'm afraid that Rodger will find out and just blow up. I don't know what to do. I'm so scared."

'Mom felt sorry for her. She knew that Ella had a big heart and was a soft touch where her customers were concerned. She often gave hard-up customers a 'discount.' She looked over the case, then told her that she was looking for a watch for Dad and wanted to buy one that was in her showcase. So, she made a down payment and bought it on layaway. Then she told Ella not to worry, because the Christmas rush would probably clear out her case. "Besides, you know that Rodger would forgive you anything. He's crazy about you."

'That cheered Ella up a bit. As the holidays loomed closer, Ella still needed to sell a lot of jewelry, and sales did pick up some with Christmas coming. The week before Christmas, she noticed the school principal breeze through the door. She perked up.

"Hi, Mr. Carlson. Are you interested in purchasing some lovely gifts for your wife and daughter? I have some beautiful pieces here that they have both been eying."

'He stopped in his tracks. "Maybe. I haven't finished my Christmas shopping yet. Let me see what you've got."

'Ella showed him a beautiful matching necklace, bracelet, and earring set, plus assorted rings and bracelets that she thought his daughter would like.

'He looked at the price tag on the necklace set. "Two hundred and eighty dollars? That's a little rich for my blood. Sorry. I think I'll look elsewhere."

'"It's high-quality jewelry. Those are semi-precious stones in real gold settings." She paused. An idea hit her. She eyed him innocently. "Well, then, maybe you'd like to purchase a nice gift for Mrs. Langford. You must be good friends as I see you visiting her quite frequently."

'Ella told Mom that he reared back, and his face nearly matched his red scarf. He looked furtively around, then snarled quietly, "What do you mean."'

'"Well, I just noticed that you seem to be on good terms since you spend so much time at her house. I thought you might like to buy her a trinket, as well as a really nice surprise for your wife and daughter. Just think, you'd have all your Christmas shopping done."'

'He looked around, then leaned over the counter and sputtered. "I-I-I'm not sure what you're getting at. We merely have PTA business to attend to. But ... but now that you mention it, it would save me some time. Which pieces do you think they might like again?"'

'He had her set aside $300 worth of jewelry. The next day he came in and paid for it in full. He picked up his packages and glared at her. "And I expect you to never mention my 'visits' to Mrs. Langford again."'

'She told Mom she looked at him, all big-eyed and innocent. "Of course not. I'm not a gossip. Lois is a good neighbor and a friend of mine. It's your business. Mum's the word." She made a lip-zipping motion and leaned forward. "And I'm sure your wife and daughter will be crazy about your gifts. Thank you for your business."

'He whirled and stomped off. She sat back and smiled. She'd made up for the money she had spent and made a tidy profit as well. Rodger would be pleased. And she would be relieved.

'She didn't quite keep her promise. She told Mom all about it and they had a good laugh. After Ella passed, Mom told me the story. I loved it.'

Sophie laughed out loud. "Serves him right, the old letch. I never did like him."

They both chuckled and lay back down and were soon asleep.

She was a member of an
old and influential
family in town.

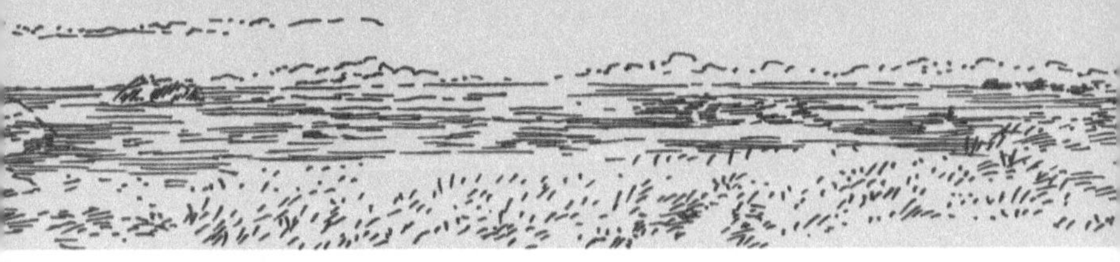

CHAPTER SEVENTEEN

MRS. RIGGERT

ALICIA WOKE in the morning with the light pouring in through the opening in the drapes over the sliding glass door of the balcony. After a long, luxurious stretch, she quietly slid out of the bed, trying not to disturb her sleeping sister where she lay in the other bed. She padded to the opening and looked out over the harbor, taking in the quiet scene as a fishing boat glided out towards the bar. She loved this view. The river swept through in a gentle curve towards the sea, its south bank lined with the sleepy old town area. To the north, the picturesque lighthouse stood erect on the lip of the sea wall, near the beginning of the sturdy stone wall of the jetty. The northern coast faded into the misty distance. She opened the balcony door and stepped out, filling her lungs with the sea air.

As she gazed down upon the quiet town, she saw a tall, slender woman walk into the cafe below. A chill raised the hair on the back of her neck. Something about the woman's rigid posture suddenly reminded her of Mrs. Riggert. She would never forget that woman.

Mrs. Riggert was the bane of all third graders. As second graders, they heard her yelling at her class through the walls.

They saw her berate cowering children in the halls and on the playground. They were all fearful of going into the third grade.

Mrs. Riggert was never seen to smile. She carried herself stiffly erect, her thin mouth grim and foreboding. She had her students cowed from the get-go. No one dared to draw her attention. It was apparent to all that she didn't like them and there was no mercy if they breached her rules. If any of them dared to draw her ire, their names would go on The List. The List meant that at the end of the day, before they left the classroom, the miscreants had to line up and bend over in turn for a swat from her wooden paddle. It hurt their pride more than it did their butts, but they feared it, nonetheless. The school board ignored the parents when they came and criticized her methods. She was a member of an old and influential family in town. So, her contract was renewed year after year.

Alicia was forced to go into Mrs. Riggert's class her third year. She spent the summer in agonized anticipation. She begged and cajoled her mother to get her changed to the other third-grade classroom, but to no avail. The school would not reassign her. The first day of school, she put on her new school dress that her mother had made, and had her mother braid her hair, so there would be no unruly hairs sticking out. Her mother handed her lunch to her as she went out the door and hugged her with encouraging words. "All you have to do is be very good and do whatever your teacher tells you, Sweetie. It will be fine. After all, they wouldn't keep her on the staff if she wasn't a good teacher."

Alicia didn't believe that for a minute. Her heart was in her throat when the bus reached the school. She ducked her head and followed the other third graders into the classroom. Mrs. Riggert stood by the door and greeted each child with a tiny, forced smile and terse instructions. "You will sit in your desk in alphabetical order. Your name is on your desk. Find it and sit quietly until everyone is seated. Brad Johnson, you're over there by the window..." And so it went until everyone was seated. The room was quiet. No "first day of school" chatter. The children looked at each other and made faces behind their teacher's back. When the bell rang, Mrs. Riggert shut the door firmly and stalked over to her desk. She sat primly on her wooden chair and went down the roll call. When everyone was accounted for, she stood up, walked to the blackboard, and wrote her name in large print. She turned to face the class.

"My name is Mrs. Riggert. If you all pay attention and follow my rules we will have a very good school year." Then she explained her rules.

"There will be no talking unless I direct you to do so. You will hold up your hand if you have a question or need to go to the bathroom. At recess you will line up at the door and proceed quietly out to the playground. At lunch, those of you who have hot lunch will proceed quietly to the cafeteria. Those of you who bring your lunch will eat at your desks."

Alicia felt dizzy with trying to remember all the rules. She twisted her hands in her lap and stared at Mrs. Riggert as her stomach flip-flopped. She was panicked with fear that she might forget a rule. As the teacher went on and on, she lost track of the rules.

They started the day by covering their books, which were on their desks, with brown wrapping paper their teacher provided. After that, the lessons commenced.

At recess the children quietly lined up and marched out to the playground. Mrs. Riggert stayed behind to work at her desk, while playground monitors took over guard duty. The children breathed sighs of relief and ran screaming on to the swings or took up impromptu ball games. Alicia ran to her friend Susan, and they laughed and chattered happily about what they had done during the summer. Finally, Alicia's face fell, and she asked Susan what she thought of their new teacher. Susan grimaced and frowned. "We'll just have to get by as best as we can. She's scary, and I don't want any trouble with her. Mamma says you're not supposed to use the word "hate" about anyone, but I can't help it. I hate her."

Allie nodded. "Me too. Her class is no fun, and she's mean." When the bell rang, they reluctantly lined up and marched back to the classroom.

Lunch hour finally came, and the lucky ones who could afford hot lunch went to the cafeteria. Allie and the rest of the class sat at their desks and quietly ate their lunches. Those whose parents had ordered it were brought small cartons of milk. Alicia eyed the cartons enviously. They had plenty of milk at home, thanks to Belle, their Jersey cow, so she had all she wanted there. But her parents couldn't afford to pay for the lunch milk. So, she would settle for a drink of water as they went out to the playground.

As the children ate, Mrs. Riggert patrolled up and down the rows, commenting on the contents of their lunch boxes. "Albert, you tell your mother that you should have fruit instead of cookies in your lunch." "David, what kind of a lunch is that? Bread and butter sandwiches and pickles? That has no nutritional value. Ask your mother to give you peanut butter sandwiches and fruit." "Marie, it looks like you have a healthy lunch. Carrot sticks are very good for you. However, you should not be bringing potato chips. Next time, bring an apple instead." And on it went.

Alicia ate as fast as she could to avoid a critique of her lunch. A peanut butter and jelly sandwich and homemade cookies were gulped down quickly. Mrs. Riggert's only comment on her lunch was a stern, "Alicia, you shouldn't eat so fast. You'll get indigestion."

Alicia felt the heat rise in her face and ducked her head. "Okay, Mrs. Riggert."

There was one little boy in the class who especially drew Mrs. Riggert's attention. Henry Folsom was small, pale and skinny, and wore horn-rimmed glasses. He also had a stuttering problem, which was always exacerbated by Mrs. Riggert's scrutiny. The other boys enjoyed picking on him or else ignored him. They called him "Sissy" and excluded him from their ball games. Alicia felt sorry for him but didn't know how to help him. Mrs. Riggert made it a point to zero in on him every day, checking his lunch and criticizing the contents.

One morning, Alicia had run out to catch the bus so fast that she forgot her lunch. When she realized her predicament, she sat silently at her desk, with tears dripping down her cheeks. What would happen to her if Mrs. Riggert found out?

Henry, who sat next to her, noticed that she wasn't eating. He leaned over, while keeping an eye on Mrs. Riggert, and whispered, "Where's your lunch?"

Alicia whispered back, "I forgot it. And Mama can't bring me one because she doesn't have a car." More tears slid down her cheeks.

Henry reached into his sack and pulled out a sandwich and surreptitiously slid half of it over to her.

"Take this. It's more than I want anyway."

Alicia's eyes grew big, and she whispered a tremulous "Thank you" to him. He grinned at her, and she grinned back. She took a bite out of the sandwich. It was delicious. Bologna! She rarely got that in her lunch. It was a real treat.

Henry continued the conspiracy by handing her half of his apple slices. Alicia was flooded with gratitude to her little friend.

Later, on the playground, she saw Henry playing alone with a ball he had brought to school. She grabbed Susan's hand and pulled her into a game of Keep Away with him and soon other kids joined in. Henry looked very happy.

But Henry began getting stomach aches at lunchtime after Mrs. Riggert would criticize his lunch, or the fact that he didn't eat all of it. Finally, Henry's mother sent a note to the school that he would be going home for lunch. Allie was relieved for Henry but missed her friend.

At recess, after lunch, the children all scattered and Alicia always headed for the swings. When she managed to snag one, she would pump herself up as high as she could. Overhead she could see the clear, blue autumn sky. This was the nicest time of year on the coast. The wind had stopped blowing and the summer fog was gone. She loved the cool, clean air of September and October.

As days went by, Allie did her best to keep a low profile. But Poor Henry couldn't seem to do anything to please Mrs. Riggert. She was impatient when he stuttered through an answer to a question, and the kids would titter as he stumbled over his words. "Yes, yes, Henry, never mind. Karen, what do you think?"

Mrs. Riggert kept a sharp eye on the boys especially, and several of them frequently made "The List" for various infractions. It became a matter of status in the male faction of the classroom. If you could take the whack of the paddle without a whimper, you were really tough. Poor Henry yelped every time, and sometimes even teared up, which made him even more of a target of the male jibes.

Alicia felt a great deal of sympathy for Henry. She thought he was nice and funny. On the freedom of the playground, he could be goofy and liked to tell silly jokes out of a joke book he had at home. She felt badly when his name went up on the board. He sometimes would say something funny in class, which would make the kids laugh. Mrs. Riggert didn't have much of a sense of humor, and his name would go up on the board for disrupting the class.

One day, at recess, Alicia sidled up to Henry and whispered in his ear. He grinned at her and nodded. At the end of the school day the miscreants were lined up to receive their punishment. When Henry's turn came, he bore the swat with stoic fortitude. The other boys were surprised and impressed. Henry stole a quick glance at Allie as she walked by and she nodded. She had suggested that Henry stuff a wad of paper towels in his shorts when he went to the boy's room. It worked.

Henry's mother was basically raising him herself, as his parents were divorced, and she was very protective of him. After a few weeks of Henry's sad reports on what went on in the classroom, she appeared at the door at the end of the day, as the children were leaving. As the last one scuttled out the door, she confronted Mrs. Riggert Alicia heard her say in a firm voice, "Mrs. Riggert, I need to have a chat with you."

After that day, Mrs. Riggert eased up on Henry a little bit. He landed on "The List" less often, but she still handed back his papers covered with red slashes and comments, and gave him low grades. Every once in a while, she would call on him to read out loud. Allie always groaned inside when that happened. Henry read poorly and stumbled over his words a lot. The harder he tried, the more he stuttered. The kids would look at each other and some would snicker. Afterwards, at recess, the other boys would make fun of him, calling him a "retard." Henry mostly played by himself then, unless some of the girls would involve him in a game.

As the year progressed, Henry became more and more withdrawn. He would find an empty corner of the playground and curl up with a book or go down the creek embankment that ran by the edge of the playground and study the plants and frogs. This was against the rules, but he managed to sneak down unobserved on occasion.

Christmas came and went, and Henry withdrew into himself even more. He stopped trying to interact with the other children and got into trouble fighting with one of the other boys at recess on more than one occasion. He was collecting a series of bruises on his arms and face.

Mrs. Riggert yelled at the boys for fighting and lined those involved up to be paddled at the end of the day. Henry stoically took his punishment, along with the rest. He seemed indifferent to the humiliation.

He looked so sad that Allie approached him on the playground at recess one day. "What's wrong, Henry? Why are you so sad?"

He was squatting on the ground next to the school building, staring at his hands. He twisted his body away from her. She persisted. "Tell me what's wrong."

He raised his fist and rubbed his eyes. "E-everybody h-hates m-me. Even m-m-my d-dad. He's g-gone away. M-m-mom says he w-won't be b--b-back."

Allie was stunned. She couldn't think of anything worse than losing her father. "Gee, I'm real sorry Henry. But I don't hate you. You're my friend. Come on and let's go swing."

He just sat with his knees drawn up to his chest and wouldn't respond. Allie hesitated, tried to coax him. "C'mon, Henry. Let's play." No response. Finally, she patted his shoulder and sadly wandered away.

One angry, gray Monday in late January, Henry was absent. As the west wind slashed the heavy raindrops against the windows, Mrs. Folsom suddenly stormed into the room. She marched up to the desk and loomed over Mrs. Riggert.

Taken by surprise, Mrs. Riggert reared back in her chair and stared at the distraught woman.

"You nasty, mean old bitch," yelled Mrs. Folsom. "Because of you, my Henry is in the hospital."

Mrs. Riggert pushed her chair back further and stood up. "Please, Mrs. Folsom. What's happened?"

"He tried to kill himself. You just couldn't let him just be a little boy who tried his best." Her voice rose to a furious pitch. "You just had to keep picking and picking and beating him down. You didn't do anything to stop the big boys from beating on him." She turned to face the class. "He tried to hang himself last night. He just couldn't take another day of torture in this class."

Mrs. Riggert put up her hand. "Mrs. Folsom, you must calm down. I'm sorry about—"

Mrs. Folsom whipped around and snarled in Mrs. Riggert's face, "What's wrong with you? Why do you teach? Do you just enjoy torturing children?"

Mrs. Riggert sputtered, "I, I assure you I do my best. They have to learn...you really shouldn't be here. You're upsetting my class...please calm down. I-I'm so sorry. Surely you can't blame me. The boy obviously has some mental issues—"

Mrs. Folsom picked up the dreaded paddle that was by the desk and waved it at the cowering woman. The children stared, mesmerized. "Don't you dare try to blame him, you sadistic witch. You have driven him out of his mind. He's terrified of you. And so are all your students."

She whipped around. "And you," she shouted at the frightened class. "What have you done to help him? Picked on him every chance you got. You bullied him and pushed him around and made fun of him. It's your fault too."

The class stared at her. Some were frightened, some were ashamed. Alicia and some of the girls were crying, and the boys looked at each other sheepishly, some stared with their mouths agape. About that time, the principal hurried into the room, the school secretary trailing behind him.

"Mrs. Folsom, please calm down. Please give me the paddle." Mr. Andrews held out his hand.

She whirled and pointed it at him. "And what did you do to help my boy? I complained to you about this bitch over and over, and you did nothing. How can you tolerate her on your staff? You know how she treats these children. My son nearly died and it's your fault as well as hers and these brats here." She waved the paddle in the direction of the students. Her face was twisted with rage, and tears streamed down her cheeks.

By now many of the children were sobbing and some of them jumped out of their seats and backed away from her.

Mr. Andrews took a step towards her. "Please, Mrs. Folsom, you're upsetting the children. Let's go to my office and sort this thing out. I'm very sorry about Henry. Let's see what we can do for him and for you. Please..." He slowly approached Mrs. Folsom, who suddenly seemed to crumble into herself. She dropped the paddle, and wept wildly, her face in her hands. He put his arm around her shoulders and carefully led her out of the room.

As they left, he turned to Mrs. Riggert. "Please come with me Mrs. Riggert. We need to sort this out. Anna will take over the classroom until we can relieve her." He looked at the secretary and nodded. With a shocked expression, she walked over to the teacher's desk and stood by it. The three adults went out the door, Henry's mother sobbing all the way.

Slowly, the class went back to their seats and came back to life. They looked at each other and started talking among themselves. Anna sat down at the teacher's desk and clapped her hands. In a firm voice she said, "Quiet, please, children. Settle down. I'm sure your teacher will be back soon. Why don't you do some reading. Get out your books and read to yourselves." Some of the girls were still sniffling, including Allie. Anna handed out tissues to them and tried to comfort them. "I'm sure Henry will be fine. His mother found him in time. Surely, he'll be back in school soon. Don't worry."

The subdued class finally settled down and, if they weren't reading, at least maintained silence. Mrs. Riggert didn't return, and later Mr. Andrews came in and relieved Anna.

A substitute teacher came in the next school day and took over the class for the next week. She got rid of the paddle, and the atmosphere in the room was much lighter and brighter.

When Mrs. Riggert returned, she proceeded as if nothing had happened. But she didn't bring back the paddle.

Word about what had happened got around town and all the sympathy was given to Mrs. Folsom and Henry. Mrs. Riggert was treated coldly by most of the townspeople who weren't related to her, and she didn't come back to teach the next year.

When Henry returned to school, the students were cautious around him. They weren't sure how to treat him. He remained aloof until, gradually, the others began to try to include him in their activities. Alicia offered him a cookie at lunch one day. He didn't look her quite in the eye but thanked her for it. Finally, some of the boys offered him a chance to play dodge ball and he soberly accepted. None of them apologized for the way they had treated him in the past, but they never picked on him again. Eventually, he even made friends with a couple of the shyer boys, and they hung out together. By the end of the school year, he seemed much more relaxed and happier.

Alicia sighed. *I wonder what ever happened to Henry. Maybe I should try to track him down.* But she knew she wouldn't. Her life was full enough as it was. She wished him well. She turned and headed for the shower, tweaking her sister's toe as she passed. "Wake up, Soph. Let's go to breakfast."

CHAPTER EIGHTEEN

LOVE AND MARRIAGE

ALICIA AND SOPHIE sat down, once again, in the Laughing Gull Cafe. A plump, gray-haired waitress came by to take their order. Allie looked up in surprise. "Chris, are you still working here? I figured you had retired long ago."

Chris looked at her in surprise. Squinting at Alicia, she did a double take. "Oh my goodness, is that you, Allie? It's been so many years since I've seen you. How're you doin?"

"Gosh, I'm fine, Chris. I retired last year. How've you been? Still married to Leonard? How are your kids?"

"Well, actually, Lennie passed away a couple years ago. The kids are grown, and I was bored. So, I came back to work."

"I'm so sorry about Leonard. I hadn't heard. I've lost contact with most of the people I know down here. It's good to see you."

Chris glanced around. "Thanks, Allie. I better stop the chit-chat and get back to work. What would you two like for breakfast?"

Allie and Sophie gave their orders and Chris took off with a brisk, "I'll be right back with your coffees."

Alicia looked at Sophie. "Wow. I can't believe she's still working here. She was working here when I was in high school. She was just two grades ahead of me, but she dropped out and eventually married. I haven't thought about her in years."

"I don't remember her at all. She was too far ahead of me in school."

Allie looked around the dining area. "I remember her and Leonard. I was surprised when they got married."

LEONARD AND CHRIS

Leonard "Buff" Bufford sat on the stool at the Laughing Gull, morosely watching Chris Larder's skinny, angular body awkwardly move about as she worked behind the counter, cleaning, dishing up ice cream, taking orders—all the usual waitress activities. Chris was tall, about five-foot-ten, skinny with a rather hooked nose, and black-framed "cat's eyes" glasses topped by lank, stringy light brown hair, which was snagged in an unattractive net. Her one redeeming feature was her beautiful, long lashed, green eyes. But she was the object of his affections. He had known her for years and was desperately in need of a girlfriend. He figured she was the perfect person for him—not too pretty but kind and non-judgmental where he was concerned.

As for Chris, she was friendly but gave him no encouragement whatsoever. When she wasn't waiting on him, she simply ignored him. She was aware of his interest in her, and was flattered, but he just wasn't what she was looking for.

He sat there, trying desperately to think of something clever to say to get her attention. He really had no idea how to approach women. His father had been removed from his life, when he was five, by a log that skidded the wrong way while being loaded on the truck. His mother alone had raised him. She had to work as a clerk at the dry goods store downtown and was always tired in the evenings. Their life together had been a quiet one, and she doted on him. But she had never taught him how to talk to girls, and now she too was gone, so he couldn't ask her.

Buff was no Rock Hudson himself. He was chubby, shorter than Chris, wore thick glasses, and had a large, bulbous nose. His unathletic body was sausaged into a gray work shirt and matching gray work pants, with heavy brown shoes on his large feet. He knew he was no "catch." He was just a lowly janitor at the nearby school, after all. But he was lonely since his mother had passed and thought he might have a chance with Chris. After all, men weren't exactly clambering to go out with her. And she had been nice to him. He had been coming here for breakfast since his mother died. And since he had overheard some guys making fun of Chris late one night.

He had dropped into one of the local bars in town, seeking the comfort of human contact. There were three rough looking, obviously drunk, local guys at a table nearby, loudly prodding each other about a girl they said was "easy." They mocked Chris's looks, each claiming that they wouldn't be caught dead "doing" her. The teasing got out of hand and the next thing he knew they started throwing punches at each other.

Bert, the owner, phoned Big Al, then came out from behind the counter with a baseball bat, ready to knock some heads. Buff sidled around the roiling group and took off out of the bar, just as Big Al came into view. On the way home, he started thinking about Chris. She had been a couple of grades behind him in school. She was mousy and not popular. She had a friend, fat, pimpled Marissa Flannery, who was unpopular too. Buff hadn't paid much attention to either of them. However, it was rumored that one of the football guys had taken a dare to have sex with Chris. Before long, she ended up pregnant. She had to leave school, her senior year, and disappeared for several months. About seven months later, she came back to town alone, and went to work in the restaurant. The guy who got her pregnant graduated with the rest of the class of '58 and went on to college on a football scholarship.

Anyway, she was available, with no prospects, and in need of a boyfriend as he saw it. Maybe he had a chance with her. Besides, he liked her eyes. And maybe those jerks were right. Maybe she would be easy to approach.

So here Chris was, waiting tables at the diner, hoping that something or someone would come along to make her life better. When Buff started showing an interest in her, she was annoyed. She told her mother about him and her mother shifted her heavy girth in her easy chair, snuffing out her cigarette in the overflowing ashtray that rested precariously on the chair arm. "You better encourage him a bit and not be so choosy. After all, who else would want you? You're tainted goods, and they all know it. He may be homely but at least he's got a steady job. As far as I know, he ain't a drinker like your father. He won't be runnin' off with some floozy from the bar."

Chris's only visible reaction was a grim tightening of her mouth. She whipped around and stalked into her bedroom, slamming the door. She sat in front of the mirror above her tiny dressing table and stared dully at her reflection.

When Jack had first shown an interest in her, she was thrilled. She'd never had a boyfriend and longed for someone, anyone, to pay attention to her. He wasn't one of the popular guys on the football team, and was actually kind of homely, with a face troubled by acne. But the guys on the team all had a certain charisma. She couldn't believe her luck. She eagerly walked right into his trap.

She was very nervous about their first date. What could they talk about? Would he really like her? What should she wear? She and her best friend, Marissa, talked excitedly over their lunch sandwiches. They discussed every aspect of her clothing choices, what she might talk about, where they might go. Marissa seemed as excited as Chris.

Chris knew her mother would never agree to her going out on a date. With no trust in men in general, and teenage boys in particular, she wanted Chris to wait until she was eighteen. Maybe by then she would have enough sense to handle them. So, she told her mother that she was going over to Marissa's house and would be back late. Then she met Jack down the street near the football stadium, where he had parked his car. She was shaking with the terror of it. He took her to a little place with a soda fountain in Coquille, away from the normal teen hangout in town, and afterwards they went to a movie at the drive-in. She tried to make conversation with him, but he wasn't much of a talker. Pretty soon, he put his arm around her, and she felt a thrill of excitement but also apprehension. He began sliding his hands down her front and soon was coming on hot and heavy, putting his hands where they didn't belong and kissing her with his tongue down her throat. She was repulsed but didn't know how to react. She was afraid to tell him to back off for fear he wouldn't like her. Her mother had warned her about men. They only wanted "one thing." And she had better not give it to them. Confused, she still accepted another invitation to go out with Jack after that, under the same secretive conditions. He dropped her off a block from her house so her mother wouldn't see. Dazed, she decided she was "in love." Maybe he would ask her to go steady. But after a couple more dates, when she had finally given in to sex, (in the backseat of his car, which was awful and messy and hurt a lot) he dropped her completely. When she tried to talk to him in the hall at school, he just ignored her and walked on.

Bewildered and hurt, she kept to herself at school, suffering deep humiliation when the boys in the hall made comments and snickered behind her back. Finally, she realized after a couple of months that her periods had stopped. Frightened and confused, in desperation, she told her mother that something was wrong. Her mother turned off her afternoon soap opera, snuffed out her cigarette, and marched her down to the doctor's office.

She endured a very embarrassing and humiliating examination, after which Dr. Maxwell pronounced her to be pregnant. Her mother turned red in the face and grew stiff as a flagpole. She grabbed Chris's arm and dragged her back out of the office. When they got home, her mother slammed the door and, turning in a rage, backhanded her so hard that her head hit the wall. She yelled at Chris, "What the hell's the matter with you? How could you do this to me? Didn't I tell ya, ya couldn't date until ya were eighteen? Didn't I tell ya to watch out for boys? You've been runnin' around behind my back. This is what comes from my trusting you. Now your life is ruined. Ruined! Who's the father? He's gonna pay for this."

Chris, sobbing, would only tell her that she didn't want to have anything to do with him. She steadfastly refused to reveal the culprit's name. She hated him and didn't want her mother causing a mess at his house with his parents. Word would get around all over town. Finally, three months later, when she was starting to show, it was arranged for her to go stay with her aunt in Springfield until she had the baby.

After all she had gone through, she lived daily with the pain of giving away her baby. She knew she was in no way able to care for her, but had wanted her, nonetheless. Her mother and aunt had insisted that Chris give her up for adoption. Finally, realizing that she had nothing to offer Lillian (the name she gave her in her mind), she gave her over to a childless couple. But she never lost the longing to hold her baby. Her life was empty. She clutched her fists to her chest as she felt the pain sweep through her once more. Maybe if she could just cuddle her baby one more time, she wouldn't hurt so much.

Gradually, she came back to the problem at hand. Maybe her mother was right. She was ugly and had no prospects. And Buff had a steady income. He could provide for her. She would give anything to get out of this crappy, moldy shack with her crazy mother and have a real home of her own. She could have another baby, and this time keep it. Maybe she should encourage him. But the thought of going through the act of sleeping with him made her skin crawl. She threw herself on the bed and wept. There was nothing in this hick town for her. She could spend the rest of her life waiting on tables here, putting up with people who treated her like dirt. She was trapped. Her mother needed her income, meager though it was. Her mother was getting by on social security at the time and had problems of her own.

She finally stopped crying and lay there thinking. Marissa had gone to beauty school in Coos Bay and was working in a salon there. They were going to go to the movies Saturday night. Maybe she would have some suggestions. She just had to get out of this place. She had to do something. Meanwhile, it wouldn't hurt to be nicer to Buff.

There was a rapping on her door. "Chrissy, Honey, are you goin' to start supper soon? You know I have to eat regular or I get fuzzy," her mother whined.

"I'm not hungry. Make yourself a sandwich."

"Oh, come on, I need somethin' hot to settle my stomach. You know that. My back is hurtin' awful. I'm just not up to it."

Chris sighed and sat up on the edge of the bed. Sometimes she hated her mother. If she could just poison the woman, she would be free to do whatever she wanted. She could move to Coos Bay or Eugene and at least have a semblance of a life. She smiled grimly to herself and walked out of the room without speaking to her mother. She slammed a skillet on the stove and fried a couple of hamburger patties for the two of them and heated some green beans out of a can. Her mother watched her from her seat at the kitchen table, puffing her Pall Malls steadily.

"You don't have to be so crabby. You're just too sensitive. I never meant to hurt your precious feelings. I was just saying the facts. We have to be practical."

Chris slapped a plate of food in front of her mother. "You've never given a damn about my feelings. All you care about is making sure I can support you. I'm going to eat in my room."

Her mother's eyes grew big and a little frightened. Chris rarely raised her voice to her like this. Chris felt a twinge of guilt, but the pent-up rage had been building up for years, and finally had to be let out. She stalked off with her plate and ate in her room while she mulled over her situation.

The next day she smiled at Buff when she set his breakfast in front of him. Pancakes and scrambled eggs and bacon. The man was nothing if not predictable. "How you doin' Buff? Looks like it'll be a nice day, huh?"

He looked startled, ducked his head and mumbled, "Yeah. Another nice day. Sure would like to go fishin.'"

"Really?" She sighed. "If I had my druthers, I'd go swimmin' at Bradley Lake. It should be fairly warmed up by now."

He blushed at the thought of Chris in a bathing suit. "Well, do you like to roller skate? Since we have to work in the daytime, maybe you'd like to go out to Tanglewood some night?"

She straightened up. "That might be fun, Buff. How about Saturday night? I haven't been out there in years and I used to love to go."

"O-oh-kay," he stuttered. "I-I could pick you up at your place at seven o'clock. Would that be all right?"

"Sure, Buff. See you then. I've got to wait on my other customers now." She whirled and went to wait on a couple in a booth by the front window.

Buff was stunned. She had actually said she'd go out with him. He was so elated, confused, and panicked he could hardly finish his breakfast. He stole glances at her while she worked. This was the longest interaction he had ever had with her. She had looked him right in the eye and smiled. He finished his meal and slipped a fifty-cent piece under his plate. He didn't want her to think he was taking advantage of their relationship by not tipping.

Energized with new vigor, he gulped, "Bye Chris," when she walked by, and he floated off to work.

That Friday, Chris went to the movies at the theater on Main Street. Since Chris didn't have a car, Marissa had to drive down from Coos Bay for their get-together. They watched Gunfight at the OK Corral, which Chris thought was too violent and boring. Then, they went to the Laughing Gull for ice cream. Over chocolate sundaes, they talked about Marissa's job and Chris' problems. Marissa enjoyed her job at the beauty parlor, and happily told Chris all about it. Then she launched into her problems with her roommate who was a slob.

She changed the subject. "You should go to beauty school too, Chris. You'd like it. Then you could get a job, and we could room together. I can't believe you're going out with Buff. But if you're going to do it, maybe you'd like me to do something with your hair? I could fix it real cute and maybe help you with a little makeup too. It'd be good for you to get out more and have someone to date. I know he's not good-looking and he's younger than you, but he always seemed nice in school. I think he's a good guy. He won't do you wrong like that other jerk. Besides, it's not like you're gonna marry him. Just go out and have some fun."

Chris was thoughtful. "Yeah, you might be right. It could be fun. You think you could give me a cool hairdo? I can't do a thing with it. I don't know about the makeup." She looked at Marissa's heavily made-up face. Her pimples were gone, but the makeup only served to emphasize her homeliness. Her over-plucked brows were drawn on in thin, dark arches. Her mascara-crusted eyelashes looked fake and lumpy, the lips too dark and intense. It just wasn't to her taste. "I'm not one for much makeup. Maybe a little lipstick."

"Let's go over to your place and have a beauty session."

Chris brightened. This could be fun. Besides, it'd be something to do. They went out into the drizzly night and headed for Chris' house. She knew her mother would be in bed, so they tiptoed cautiously into Chris' bedroom and set up shop. Using a set of sewing shears, Marissa managed to cut Chris' hair into a short, sassy bob. Shampooed and blown dry, it took on new life and shone nicely in a style that gave Chris' thin face a perky, hip look. She loved it.

They next experimented with some of Marissa's makeup, erupting into giggles every few minutes while Chris shushed Marissa for fear of waking her mother. Chris decided that she needed some lipstick and maybe eye shadow. Marissa offered to pluck her eyebrows, but she decided that she could do that herself. She didn't want to take a chance on Marissa getting carried away. She would pick up some eye shadow the next morning at the pharmacy. She looked at herself in the mirror and smiled. Wow! She looked almost attractive. Maybe there was hope for her yet. She hugged Marissa and thanked her profusely.

Marissa giggled and looked very pleased with herself. "It was nothing. It was fun. You look so cute now. I should've done this a long time ago..."

The next evening when Buff stopped by to pick her up, he was surprised to see her new hairstyle and the green eye shadow emphasizing her green eyes. He felt flattered that she had gone to the effort for him, and nervous at the same time. He politely said, "Hello," to her mother, as she eyed him up and down. After a short exchange of "How are you," and "Nice to meet you," the couple escaped out the door. He held the car door open for Chris, like she was a delicate princess, and walked around the car. He drove on out to Tanglewood along the winding coastline in a daze. He turned on the radio to the only station he could get and the sounds of Elvis' "Blue Suede Shoes" blasted the air. He quickly turned down the volume and searched for something to say.

"You like Elvis?" Well, it was a start.

"Oh yeah, he's my favorite. And Pat Boone and the Four Seasons and Connie Francis. Who're your favorites?"

"I like all of 'em. Rock 'n Roll in general, but most anything. I like country too."

The rest of the drive they talked about their favorite music and before they knew it, they were turning into the parking lot of the huge, brightly lit skating rink. Chris felt a stir of excitement. She loved skating. Maybe this would be fun after all. But she hoped nobody she knew would see them there. She was a little embarrassed by her homely escort.

As they entered the building, the sound of music and the flashing lights gave her a thrill and she felt eager to get out on the floor. They picked up their skates at the counter, placed their shoes and her purse in a locker, and, after donning their skates, pushed out on the floor. The sensation of rolling along as they picked up speed made Chris' pulse pick up. For a while they skated quickly around the broad floor to the beat of the rock music. Soon the voice over the loudspeaker boomed that it was time for a couples' slow skate. Surreptitiously, Buff wiped his hand dry on his shirt, and took Chris' hand as they sailed on around the floor. Soon some of the couples were doing tricks and dancing, whirling around them. Buff turned to Chris. "D-do you want to do the waltz? It's fun. I used to do it with my mom when I was little." He blushed deeply.

Chris looked confused. "I don't know. I've never done that before. I don't want to make a fool of myself."

Buff smiled his sweet smile. "Can you skate backwards? Or do circles? If you can do that you can waltz."

"Okay. Let's try it. But don't be surprised if we both land on the floor."

They slowed down as Buff turned to face her, assumed the waltz position, and gently began to steer her around. They moved unsteadily for a while, until they hit the rhythm of it, and were soon whirling around the floor.

Chris' serious face softened, and soon they were both laughing as they corrected missteps but managed to stay on their feet. They spent the next hour going through the various commands of the loudspeaker, as the music changed and the moves became more complex. They did end up on the floor a couple of times but wound up unhurt and laughing. Chris couldn't remember when she'd had this much fun. She realized that she enjoyed being with Buff. She could be herself with him. After all, she wasn't going to marry him. She didn't have to worry about making an impression. They were just friends. And he was so gentle with her.

After leaving the rink they stopped at the Laughing Gull for ice cream sodas. They sat across from each other in the booth and Buff wracked his brain for something to talk about. Chris surprised him by starting the conversation. "Buff, that was the most fun I've had in years. Thanks for taking me."

His face turned red, and he grinned. "Gosh, I thought the same thing. I'd forgotten how much I enjoyed skating. Maybe we can do it again soon."

"I'd like that. You're a nice person, Buff. I feel like we could be good friends."

He ducked his head. "Me too. What d'you like to do besides swimming and skating?"

"Believe it or not, I like to go clamming, and to the movies. I like to read too. Just about anything I can get my hands on."

"Me too. Since my mom died, I haven't felt like getting out much. I still do the short-wave radio stuff with my buddies. But I'd love to go to a movie with you. How about next Saturday?"

Chris hesitated. She didn't want him to think she didn't have anything else going on in her life, even if she didn't. "I'll have to check my calendar and get back to you on that. It seems like I had something coming up next weekend, but I can't remember what. But a movie would be nice."

When Buff took her home, he politely escorted her to the door. Chris turned and held out her hand. "Thanks so much, Buff. It was a lot of fun. We'll do it again soon. I'll let you know about Saturday."

Buff shyly shook her hand and smiled. "Thank you, Chris. It was fun for me too."

She smiled. "Good night, then. See you soon." Turning away, she let herself in the door.

Buff floated back to his car and drove off.

The next few weeks, they went out together several times. Chris began to realize how much she enjoyed doing things with Buff and couldn't believe the courtly way he treated her. He never tried to force himself upon her. No one had ever shown such regard for her, other than Marissa. She grew to respect him and realized that he was as lonely as she was. He began to look less homely to her.

Then one day a young man came into the cafe. Chris looked up and saw a blonde-haired, blue-eyed, well-muscled Greek god. She felt a thrill of excitement. Then caught her reflection in the mirror and her homeliness slapped her in the face. No one like him would ever be interested in her. She blushed deeply, drew in a deep breath, and turned to face him at the counter. "What can I get you?" she gasped.

He looked her in the eye and smiled. Chris was dazzled. "I'm starved. I'd love a burger and fries, and maybe a chocolate shake."

Chris croaked, "Comin' right up." She whirled and snapped the order on the wheel in the window between the counter and the kitchen. Then she busied herself making the shake. She pulled the metal cup from the blender and poured the shake into a tall glass, then placed it in front of him. She plastered on her best smile. "What brings you to our little town? I don't think I've seen you in here before."

He smiled a slow, warm smile her way and leaned his elbows on the counter. "I'm the new assistant coach at the high school. Also, part-time science/P.E. teacher. I came down to look for an apartment and get set up before school starts. Do you go to the high school?"

Her face went hot again. "No. My class graduated two years ago. I've worked here ever since."

He held out his hand. "I'm Jared Brown. What's your name?"

Still blushing, she shook his hand briefly and stammered, "Um, Chris. Chris Larder. Um, welcome to Bandon."

"Thanks. You wouldn't know where there might be a good, inexpensive apartment available, would you?"

"I'm afraid not. But you might look in the Western World ads. We have one here." She pulled the paper out from under the counter where she had stashed it, pleased with herself for putting it there. She handed it to him.

He gave her a lopsided grin. "Thanks. I owe you." He opened the paper to the ads and began poring over them.

Chris went self-consciously on with her work, wiping down the counter and cleaning off a booth table. What a dreamboat. And he wasn't wearing a wedding ring. She had checked on that. This was so exciting. Soon the cook rang the bell for his order, and she carefully handed it to him.

He looked up from his paper, smiled a "Thanks," her way, and delved into the food while he bent back over the ads. He pulled his pen out of his shirt and circled some of them.

Chris hesitated. "Would you like a glass of water?"

"Huh? Oh, yeah. That'd be good. Thanks."

She placed the glass in front of him and went on wiping down tables, taking orders from a couple who came in. She watched him out of the corner of her eyes. He was so good-looking. Don't get your hopes up, Chris, she told herself. *"He's way out of your league."* But it didn't hurt to look.

More customers came in and she did her job with a distracted air. She messed up a couple of orders and got snapped at by the customers and the cook. She was keenly aware of his presence as she moved around.

Charlene, the evening shift waitress, finally walked in and Chris' heart sank. Charlene was twenty-six, a bleached blond with a dynamite figure, and divorced. Chris knew Charlene would immediately make a play for Jared.

Charlene bounced into the back, hung up her coat, and put on the white apron that passed for waitress' uniforms. As she walked back out to the front, she did a double-take at the sight of Jared. She looked at Chris, rolled her eyes, and mouthed, "Wow." She sashayed up to Jared, smiled seductively, and asked, "Is there anything else you need?"

He looked up, startled, and politely said, "No thanks. I'm just about done."

She reached for his empty plate. "Let me clear this away for you. If there's anything else you want, just let me know."

"Where'd Chris go? She's been real helpful."

Charlene pouted. "I'm afraid you'll have to put up with me. Chris' shift is over."

Chris slid into the kitchen and then the back room to sign out from her shift. She put on her coat and slipped out the back door. Walking home, her thoughts were glum. She would never stand a chance with a guy like that. The best she would ever do would be Buff, or someone like him. Her future was bleak.

The next two weeks, Jared came in every day for lunch. Chris always tried to think of something to say. "Did you find an apartment?" opened the door to a discussion of where to find necessities such as toiletries, furniture, and so on. She was thrilled to guide him to the best places to get it all. Some furniture could be purchased cheaply through the want ads. He told her all about his acquisitions for furnishing his place. They developed an easy rapport. Chris began to have dreams about him.

When Buff came in for his usual breakfast, he noticed that Chris was not as attentive as she had been. He wondered if he had done something wrong. When he asked her to go to the movies with him, she said she had "Something else planned and couldn't go that weekend, but thanks for asking."

Buff wracked his brain, trying to figure out what was going on. But he continued coming in for breakfast anyway.

One day he popped in for lunch as a surprise for Chris. There she was, laughing and chatting with a handsome stranger. Buff was filled with a hot surge of jealousy and spun around and left, his morale shattered.

The next few days Buff steered clear of the diner. He was sure that the new guy had stolen his girl. He felt like his life was over. He really liked Chris and had hoped that she liked him too. But he didn't stand a chance with the new guy.

Chris noticed Buff's absence but was too besotted to pay attention to it. She was so enthralled by Jared, and he was so nice to her. He even was encouraging her to get her GED. She was seriously looking into it. She went to the high school office to ask how to go about it. They gave her the information and she took it home to peruse at her leisure.

Then Jared dropped the bomb. "My fiancée will be coming down next weekend to check out the apartment."

Chris shriveled inside. "Your fiancée?"

He grinned. "Yeah, we were putting off getting married until she finished up her degree. I can't wait to see her."

Chris bit her lip to keep it from trembling, turning her back to pick up the coffee pot to replenish his cup. "That's great. Congratulations."

He didn't notice her distress and kept babbling on about his betrothed while the words just didn't penetrate Chris' head. He was taken. He had never mentioned a woman in his life until now. She was furious with him and with herself for ever dreaming about him.

The next day she called in sick to work and stayed home. She sulked in her room, ignoring her mother's whining enquiries. What an idiot she was. How could she even dare to think she could attract a man like Jared. All the time he was just being friendly.

She went back to work without enthusiasm and went through the motions of her job. All of a sudden, she missed Buff. Why hadn't he been coming in lately?

That night she called him. "Hi, Buff. Where have you been? I've missed you on the breakfast shift."

His voice was cold. "I didn't think you would notice, since you have that handsome guy hanging all over you."

"What guy? You mean Jared? He's just a friend. He's the new assistant coach at the high school. I've just been telling him about the town. He comes in every day for lunch. You don't have to worry about him, he's engaged. I'm entitled to have friends, aren't I? Besides, you don't own me, Buff. I didn't realize you were the jealous type."

There was a pause. Then, humbly, "Gosh, I'm sorry. I just thought you were interested in the guy. I haven't dated much, and I thought we had something special going."

"We do. We're good friends. Who knows where that might lead? Come back for breakfast tomorrow and maybe we can get together this weekend."

"I'd like that." His voice was warm again. "See you tomorrow."

Three months later, they were married in a quiet ceremony at the local First Southern Rite Holy Baptist Church of Christ. There were only a handful of people in attendance. Chris' mother was happy. Marissa was happy. Buff's old school chums were happy. Buff was ecstatic. They all thought that Chris' tears were tears of joy.

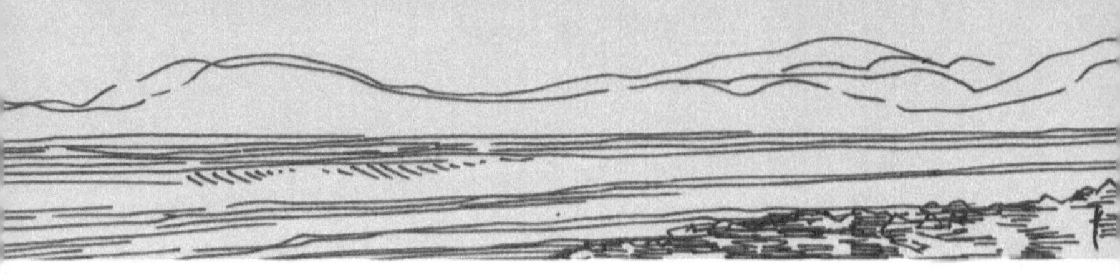

CHAPTER NINETEEN

VIOLET
GANTLER

AFTER BREAKFAST, Allie and Sophie took one last drive past their old school, and on through the Beach Loop as they returned to the motel to pack. On their way by the school Allie suddenly thought about one of her favorite teachers. "Did you have Mrs. Gantler for English, Sophie?"

"Yeah. Man, she was strict. But I liked her class. She was fair and we learned how to diagram sentences and got to read a lot. She treated us all the same, even the worst students."

"I just loved her class. She really encouraged me in my writing and reading more advanced stuff than the rest of the class. She got me reading the Bronte sisters, and Poe and Hemingway. Lots of things I might not have picked out on my own. She told me that I had to read a lot to live up to my potential."

Sophie sighed. "I guess she's gone now, too. Most of our old teachers are. Makes me feel old to think about it."

"Yeah. I think she stayed here after she retired until she passed away."

The women were quiet, remembering, as the car glided one last time past the magnificent shoreline.

VIOLET'S STORY

Violet Gantler was built like a bulldog. She was short, big bosomed, a little bow-legged, and stout. She wore rayon dresses, or skirts and vests with sturdy, black old-lady shoes. Her hairstyle was still stuck in the 40s, rolled back from her forehead with a bun on the back of her head. Her aristocratic, sharp nose perched on a sagging, round face that dissolved into jowls, adding to the bulldog look. But she kept herself neat and primly made up for her professional image. She always smelled faintly of lavender.

Violet taught English and literature at the high school to the freshmen and sophomores. Nobody messed with Mrs. Gantler. She could freeze an entire class with a stern frown from behind her cat's-eye's glasses. When she lowered her head, went dead silent, and glowered over the tops of those glasses, the students knew they were in trouble. Perhaps there would be an extra essay, or another book added to the list they had to read and report on. They would immediately go quiet and sit at attention. The worst miscreants were simply sent to the office. She had an unassailable aura that few of them dared to disrespect.

Some of the students made fun of her when she wasn't around. But the ones who wanted to learn liked her and didn't give her any trouble. She made them work hard. She loved to read to her classes, giving voice to the text in a dramatic way that held their attention. She made them diagram sentences and write essays and book reports. Some of them, mostly girls, enjoyed that and wrote copiously. Many of the others didn't and their work showed it. Violet marked their papers as needed and graded according to merit. She gave praise where it was due, made suggestions for improvement, and F's where deserved. In the 50s, parents didn't question the grades their kids received. Her ruling was law.

Violet lived alone. Her beloved Benjamin had passed away from cancer when he was only forty. While their marriage had been less than passionate physically, they had been good friends and companions. They met in college, and shared their interests in literature and art. Their courtship had been primly proper. The bespectacled Benjamin, also a teacher, had been suitably kind and gentle, and she had liked him very much. She had been raised to be a lady and was a virgin when they got married, as was he. Sex was a necessary burden, and she tried to pretend she enjoyed it for his sake. He didn't ask her for it too often. She was sad that no children ever came of it. Then he had died, and she wasn't interested in re-marrying. She stayed on in her little house with her three cats. Dogs were too rowdy and messy, whereas her cats were sweet, quiet, mostly, and buried their poop neatly in the litter box, which she kept in the utility room.

She missed her husband terribly after he died. They could bounce ideas off of each other and discuss any subject that came up. She desperately missed the companionship. But she was used to being on her own now, doing as she pleased. She made the best of it. She had friends among the teachers. Her closest friend was Betty Ferris, who taught sixth grade.

Violet attended the First Southern Rite Holy Baptist Church of Christ most Sundays. A familiar figure in the congregation, she was a trusted member of the community. People gobbled up the sour cream chocolate cake she always brought to every potluck dinner.

Fond of her students, she followed their progress through the school with interest. Her busy life included looking after her parents, now in their late eighties, who lived a few blocks away.

Every Saturday night, it was her habit to dine at the Laughing Gull Cafe on the hill. The outgoing waitresses were kind and the tiny cook, "Reenie," was usually joking with the help. They all knew Violet, greeted her with smiles, and took her right away to the table by the window which was her favorite. They always asked her how she was as if they really cared, which made her feel special. She usually ordered fish and chips, followed by a chocolate sundae. Even when the place was bustling with activity they managed to serve her quickly.

All in all, her life was comfortable and it suited her. Being a teacher in a small-town high school fit her ambitions. Except for one. She harbored a secret desire to be a writer. She was a great admirer of the classics, but also loved the more modern writers—Steinbeck, Fitzgerald, Hemingway. She wanted to write like them. In her spare time, she sat at her typewriter and wrote short stories and romantic novels, for which she had a huge pile of rejection slips. She didn't understand why nobody wanted to publish her work, but that didn't stop her. Occasionally, she would ask Betty to critique something before she sent it to the publisher. Betty sometimes had constructive criticism but praised her writing profusely. She kept on writing. It gave her life a purpose other than teaching. It made her feel hopeful and important. Someday, someone would recognize the beauty of her words.

Sometimes she assigned a short essay for the students, giving them a subject, or a line from a play to expand upon. Some of them groaned when she did this, but she was unmoved by their complaints.

One day, she assigned a passage from Shakespeare's Hamlet, which the class had been studying: "To be, or not to be: that is the question. Whether 'tis nobler in the mind to suffer the slings and arrows of outrageous fortune, or to take arms against a sea of troubles and, by opposing, end them."

The students looked at her blankly. Shakespeare was a foreign language to them. One girl timidly raised her hand. Violet nodded at her. "Yes, Elizabeth?"

"What does that mean? I don't get it."

Violet sighed. This girl didn't "get" so many things. How many times had she gone over that passage, trying to explain it to them. She stifled her irritation. "Hamlet is asking whether it is better 'to be,' in other words to live, when life is miserable or hard, and to fight through our troubles, or to 'not be'...to die. I want you to tell me your reaction to that. Surely you have some thoughts on the subject of life and death."

She couldn't tell from their generally sullen or blank expressions whether they understood or not. Well, she would find out when they handed in their papers.

She collected the papers on Friday and hauled them home after work. The next day she went through them, carefully. She marked down for misspellings and grammatical errors. Some of the papers were short and laughable. Elizabeth wrote, "I think it's better to be than not to be because I don't want to be dead. When you're dead you are stuck in the ground and all smelly and icky. I would rather be. Whatever the problem is, you just have to get help. I'd ask my mother if I was in trouble."

Some were more thoughtful and intelligently written. Some were sprinkled with big words, meant to impress. But when she came to Frederick Murphy's paper, she stopped at the end of the first paragraph. Her lips tightened, and she sat up in her chair. Slowly she reread the sentences.

Frederick was one of her more troubled students. He sat in the back of the class, mute and sullen. Sometimes she called on him just to be sure he wasn't asleep. He wore battered jeans, and plaid flannel shirts, with beat-up tennis shoes and no socks. He was nearly six-feet tall and had a head of greasy black hair that badly needed to be cut. She noticed that he didn't seem to have any friends. She never saw him laughing or chatting with the other students. Once he came to class with a huge black eye. When she asked him about it, he muttered that he had walked into a door. It was rumored that his father was a mean drunk. And there were stories about Frederick drinking with his drop-out buddies on the weekends. She had seen him wandering around town late at night when she was driving home from a movie or a meeting. Yet, he always got A's and B's on his tests. When she asked him questions, his answers were brief but correct, and his papers were usually well thought out.

But this time, his paper set off alarm bells. "To be or not to be." I think it's better not to be. Sometimes you get so tired of 'taking arms against a sea of troubles.' Sometimes you think it's not worth the fight. You think it would have been a whole lot better if you'd never been born. What's the use of fighting if life isn't worth living? Yes, it's better to 'not be.'

'Not being would be so peaceful and quiet. You wouldn't have to worry about anything or anyone. It would be easy. Much easier than fighting through a 'sea of troubles.' Especially if there isn't any possible way to fight them."

Brief and to the point, but poignant. This boy was in serious trouble. This was a cry for help. This was something beyond what she'd ever encountered before. She'd had troubled kids in the past, but nothing this bad. What should she do?

She called the principal, Alec Reed, and set up an appointment to meet with him before school on Monday.

They met in his office, and she outlined her concerns. He looked at her with troubled eyes. Worry lines crisscrossed his forehead and deepened around his mouth. "That boy has a terrible home life. According to rumor, his father is a nasty drunk and beats his wife and kids." He shifted in his seat and clasped his hands. "I can call the CPS, but they're so overloaded that it could be a while before they get to the problem. There are so many cases like this. I'll call them, but I'll have a talk with Frederick myself and see if I can figure out what's going on. I'll see if I can get to the bottom of it."

Violet swallowed her doubts and, still troubled, proceeded to her classroom. When she handed back the papers to her class, she bent over and said softly, "Frederick, I would like to see you after your last class today. Please come by my room. And don't worry, you're not in trouble."

He looked at her out of the corner of his eyes and mumbled, "Okay."

After her last class she sat at her desk and tried to grade papers, waiting for him to show up. She felt sweaty and nervous. Sometimes teens were so secretive and hard to reach. She got up and lowered the blinds against the strong afternoon sun. She paced back and forth behind her desk, then sat and stared at the paper in front of her. Finally, after half an hour, Frederick ambled into the room.

"You wanted to see me? I can't stay long. I have to get home and do my chores."

She looked at him and paused. Folding her hands in front of her, she shifted in her chair and spoke. "Frederick, please take a seat."

After he had done so, she again hesitated. She cleared her throat and got to it. "Frederick, I am concerned about your paper. It seems to me that you're in trouble. You appear to be very depressed."

He was fiddling with his hands, not looking at her. "I'm okay. Can I go now?"

"Frederick, if you're in trouble, you need to talk to someone who can help you. Perhaps Principal Carlton. Or even me. I'm always here to listen."

She watched him sit stiffly in his seat for a minute, his long legs tucked beneath him. His gaze never left the floor. "All right, Frederick. If you don't want to talk about it, I can't make you. But if there is anything I can do to help you, please feel free to call on me. And remember," again she cleared her throat. "If you're having difficulties, you only have a year and a half of school to go and then you can go out on your own. Don't you think you can stand anything for a year and a half? I know it seems like a long time, but you'll find it goes much faster than you think right now."

"Yeah, I guess. Thanks."

Her voice was pleading. "You're a good student. I see a lot of potential in you. Please don't do anything rash. I want to see you graduate. There are people who care about you, including me." She paused for a moment. He didn't reply. "Okay, you're free to go. I'll see you in class. Take care."

He left quickly, slipping quietly out the door. She stayed on for a while, pondering what she might have said differently to reach him. Should she have offered to speak to his parents? That might just make things worse. Perhaps she should have given him the phone number of Children's Services. If only the school had trained counselors for troubled students. Finally, she sighed, packed up her papers and left for home.

The school year ended. Two weeks later, the local paper ran an article on the front page with Frederick's picture. He had disappeared. Violet's knees gave out and she sat down hard at her kitchen table. He'd had a terrible row with his father and knocked him out with a chunk of stove wood. The man had to be taken to the hospital by ambulance. After that, Frederick had fled. His distraught mother had called the police.

Most people, including the police, thought he'd run away. But Violet feared something much more sinister. What if he had done himself in? She prayed that it wasn't so. She called the police station and asked if there was any word on the boy. She was told that there wasn't a trace of him, and he had been reported as a runaway. She hung up with a feeling of dread.

The following Monday, she received yet another rejection slip in the mail. they were nice about it, saying that she had a lovely way with words but not enough drama and tension. Now she was really depressed. Nobody wanted her words. They hadn't helped Frederick, and now he was missing.

What was she going to do with her life? She was tired of trying to get published. She needed to find something more rewarding to do when she wasn't working. She was done with writing, at least for now.

I need to get away for a while, she thought. *It's been at least two years since I've gone anywhere. A road trip would be fun.* She glanced at the picture of her widowed sister, Rose, that sat on her desk. They rarely saw each other, since she lived in San Francisco. Violet would drive down to see her. Rose was living alone now that her two children were married, and she was getting up in years. Also, Violet's car was nearly new and had never been on a long trip. This would give her a chance to really break it in.

She immediately dialed her sister. After several rings, Rose picked up the phone. "Hello?"

"Rose dear, it's Violet. How are you?"

"It's so nice to hear from you." Then came the ailment litany. "I'm fine, except for my arthritis in my knees and hips. And my high blood pressure. And that bunion on my right big toe is driving me crazy. How are you?"

Violet bit her lip. Rose's glass was always half empty. One of the reasons they seldom spoke. "I'm well. I was thinking that I'd come down to see you. It's been so long, and I have a few weeks off. I thought I'd drive down next Monday. I'd stop overnight along the way and that would put me at your place sometime Tuesday afternoon. Would that be convenient for you?"

After a slight hesitation, Rose replied, in a raspy monotone. "That would be great. It's been such a long time since we got together. Do come."

Violet felt deflated. Rose had never been able to embrace their personality differences. They would never be close.

But Rose was all the family she had. She had to try to keep the channels of communication open.

"I thought I'd ask my friend, Betty, to come with me. I hate to drive that far by myself. Would you be able to put the two of us up for a few days?"

Another pause. "Um, of course, if you don't mind sharing the guest room."

"Great. Thanks, Rose. I'll call her up right away and get back to you."

That decided, she called her best friend, Betty. Betty was a spinster who taught the sixth grade at the Harbor Lights Grade School. They had been best friends for ten years. Violet was sure she could persuade her to come along.

Betty answered the phone on the first ring with a musical, "Hellooo."

Violet smiled. "Betty, I've just decided to drive to San Francisco next week to visit my sister. Why don't you come with me? It'd be such fun. The restaurants there are great, and Chinatown is fun and there are lots of sights to see. And perhaps we could throw in a side trip to Yosemite while we're at it."

"Ohmygosh! I'd love to do that. I've never been to San Francisco. Or Yosemite. Would we be staying at your sister's?"

"Yes, for two or three nights. We'll stop overnight on the way going there and back. We could share the cost of the rooms and gas. We both need a break. When was the last time you had a vacation?"

"It's been forever. I have some savings I could use. This is exciting. Let's do it."

Violet felt a small bolt of irritation at that. Of course, Betty had more than enough savings to go. She was tight as a tick. "Let's get together and make plans." They decided to meet for lunch the next day at the Laughing Gull Cafe.

Feeling a spark of excitement, Violet got out the map of California. Yes, they would take highway 101 south, spend the night in Arcata, and continue on down 101 to San Francisco. It would be a beautiful drive through the Redwoods and then on to the Bay. She felt a surge of adrenaline as the excitement began to build. Why hadn't she thought of this before? It was just what she needed.

The following Monday at 7 A.M., she pulled up in front of Betty's house. Betty, tall, awkward, wearing turquoise blue knit slacks and matching jacket, came huffing out of her house. Her grey permed hair bounced wildly around her round, cheerful face. She pulled an enormous suitcase behind her, along with an overnight case, with a huge beige purse and overcoat slung over her arm. They managed to get all the luggage into the trunk of Violet's black and white '55 Ford sedan and slammed the lid down. The rest was thrown into the back seat.

"Just a minute. I've got a couple of more things," Betty proclaimed. She dashed into her house, came back out the door, locked it and lugged a large picnic basket back to the car.

"Isn't this exciting?" she beamed. "I brought us lunch so we could picnic in one of the parks along the way. Also, snacks in case we get hungry."

"That's a great idea. I enjoy picnics when there aren't too many bugs." Violet suspected that Betty just didn't want to pay for lunch in a restaurant but liked the idea anyway. In spite of Betty's sometimes annoying ways, Violet loved her always upbeat, bright and cheery chum.

The drive down was a great success. They were almost giddy with the freedom of the road, laughing and giggling like schoolgirls. They lunched in a lovely seaside park along the way, where they could watch the waves washing in on the beach, then drove on to Arcata. Violet was anxious to find a motel with rooms available, but most of them were full. Finally, they found one with a "Rooms Available" sign and, relieved, Violet pulled in.

Betty looked at the place and said, "It looks expensive."

Violet was impatient. "It's the only one I could find. We'll just have to bite the bullet."

Betty was unhappy over the price of the room, $75, and tried to haggle with the clerk about it, but he stood firm. Violet, embarrassed by all the fuss, snapped, "We'll take it." She glared at Betty and smiled sweetly at the clerk, thanked him for the keys, and led the way to their room. They shared a room with a double bed and a hide-a-bed. They flipped a coin for the hide-a-bed and Violet got stuck with it. She was so tired that she fell immediately asleep as soon as her head hit the pillow, anyway.

The next morning, after breakfasting at a nearby cafe, they were on their way again. The drive through the Redwoods was awe-inspiring. They stopped frequently to take pictures and just walk under the gigantic trees. Violet felt her tensions and worries melt away under that cool, green canopy. Betty was equally impressed and exclaimed over the sheer size and beauty of the forest. Violet was glad to have Betty there to share the experience.

The drive on down 101 to San Francisco was beautiful and uneventful, except when they stopped for gas. They had agreed to take turns paying for the gas as they went. When it was Betty's turn, she watched anxiously for the cheapest gas prices along the road. Violet finally pulled into a station when the tank was getting low, Betty reminded her that they could have saved five cents per gallon at one they had passed. Violet gritted her teeth. "Sorry, Betty, but this is where we're running out of gas."

When they finally reached the Golden Gate Bridge, Betty sat up in her seat. "Oooh, look, Violet. Isn't it beautiful? Look at the boats and how blue the water is. It's gorgeous! And there's the city. It's so exciting."

Violet's heart soared. "Well, you'll have to be my eyes while I'm concentrating on my driving. But it really is beautiful. Now, I hope we can find Rose's place. You have to be my co-pilot. She gave me instructions and we have the city map, so tell me which way I need to turn at least a block before I need to do it. The traffic's awful, and I'm not used to it." She clutched the steering wheel in her sweaty hands and sat very straight in her seat.

Betty frowned at the map. "Okay, we have to turn left two blocks up." After several hair-raising turns and backtracking three times, they finally came to a stop in front of Rose's lovely, small Victorian home. They pulled into the narrow driveway that led to the single-car garage.

Rose greeted Violet on the vine-covered, wide front porch, with a polite hug and a big smile. "It's so lovely to see you, Violet. It seems like forever." She had never been an effusive person.

She shook Betty's hand when Violet introduced her and led them into the living room. The room was furnished with antiques and looked stiff and uncomfortable. Nothing had been changed since she last saw it. The bay window was encased in deep green velvet drapes, the walls covered with flowered wallpaper, the wood furnishings gleamed. There was an elaborate, mahogany and glass case that held delicate China bric-a-brac and an elegant tea set. The straight-backed sofa and chairs did not invite lounging. Rose waved her hand, "This is the parlor, as you can see. Now let me show you to your room."

Rose led them up the narrow stairs and down the hall to their room. More antiques. There was a double bed with an ornate, oversized headboard. The antique oak dresser and nightstands nearly filled the rest of the room. Rose pointed out the small closet. "You can hang your clothes in there. I'm sorry I only have the double bed. I hope you'll be comfortable."

"It's lovely, Rose. We'll be fine. We're grateful that you can put us up." They plopped their bags inside the door. Violet looked at Betty. "Let's unpack later. Rose, would you like to show Betty around the house? She'll need to know where things are. And I really need to use the bathroom."

Rose was pleased to give Betty a tour. There was her own bedroom, a sewing room, and the bathroom upstairs. Downstairs were the "parlor," dining room, kitchen with a large pantry, and a powder room. Betty "oohed" and "ahhed" over the antiques. The house really was a time capsule. Rose had lived there for forty-five years. It was 3:30 in the afternoon and Rose offered tea and cookies to tide them over until dinner.

They enjoyed their refreshments, helped Rose clean up, and went upstairs to unpack. Once in their room, Betty giggled and asked Violet if she thought they could sleep in the same bed comfortably. Violet shrugged and told her they would have to make do, unless Betty would like to go to a hotel? Betty coughed and decided it would all work out fine and they settled in.

The next day turned out to be one of those beautiful San Francisco summer days. Violet, feeling invigorated by the sun, invited Rose to go sight-seeing with them. She declined, pleading sore knees and hips. Perhaps they could all go out to dinner when the women got back.

The friends had a long list of things to see and ordered a cab to take them downtown. First on the list was Union Square, followed by a cable car ride, and then to Fisherman's Wharf. They left the taxi at the Square and set out to explore the shops nearby. As they crossed the square, Violet noticed people sitting around with begging cups in front of them. It shocked her. Were they in India? She tried not to stare but couldn't help glancing at them. Most of them just sat on the sidewalk with some sort of container in front. Many of them had signs, 'Out of work, any amount helps,' and such. She thought the majority of them looked like hippies. The sight of one beggar stopped her in her tracks. There was something familiar about his large frame and greasy black hair as he hunched over, hiding his face from view. She stepped up to him. "Frederick?" The man didn't move. "Frederick?" Louder this time. Still no response. She reached down and tapped him on the shoulder. Finally, he slowly raised his head. She gasped. Yes, it was her missing pupil. She glanced at Betty, who was staring in astonishment, mouth agape, and shook her head slightly. She bent over her long-lost student.

"Frederick," she began gently, "what are you doing here? How did you get here?"

He stared at her, fear in his eyes. "You won't tell anyone you saw me, will you?"

"Frederick, you need to explain yourself. I'm sure your mother is worried to death about you. Why did you run away?"

He glanced around and muttered, "I can't talk here."

"There's a restaurant across the street. Why don't you let me buy you a meal and tell me what's going on?"

Again, he glanced around. "Promise not to rat on me?"

"I promise. Let me at least get a hot meal into you and we'll talk."

Slowly, moving stiffly like an old man, he got up, swayed a bit, and followed her and Betty to the restaurant. At the entrance, Violet turned to Betty and politely suggested that perhaps she would like to check out the department store next door while she visited with her student. Betty, eyebrows raised, nodded agreement. "That's a good idea. I'll meet you back here in forty minutes. Is that all right?"

"Great. See you then." Relieved, Violet led the way to a table against the wall, towards the back of the room. When the waitress came with the menus, she ordered a cup of coffee. Then, she watched Frederick as he looked over the menu and ordered the biggest breakfast they had, plus a hamburger and coffee. He glanced at Violet to see if that was all right. She smiled and nodded. *My God, he's so thin*, she thought. *I hope he's not sick.* She was dismayed to see how rough he looked. He had deep shadows under his eyes, his jacket was dirty and torn, as was the t-shirt he wore under it. There was a new scar on his left cheek. And he simply stunk. She sat back in her chair, inhaling her coffee.

She noticed his hands. The nails were rimmed in black. "Frederick, why don't you use their facilities to wash up a bit before you eat?"

He ducked his head in embarrassment. "Yeah, I could use some soap and water. Excuse me." He headed for the men's room.

When he returned, it was obvious that he'd washed his face and his hair as well as his hands. Violet was moved. As soon as he settled, she got directly to the point. "Now, please tell me how you got here and where you intend to go. Why are you doing this?"

His eyes welled up. He didn't say anything for a long time. She could see that he was struggling not to cry, swallowing the lump in his throat as he stared into space. Finally, he burst out with a hoarse whisper. "I think I killed my dad. He was whaling on my mom, and I just couldn't take it anymore and I hit him as hard as I could with a chunk of firewood. When he went down, I hit him a couple of times more, just to be sure he wouldn't get back up. I was so scared. I grabbed a couple hundred bucks I'd saved and my coat and ran. I hitch-hiked all the way down here. My money didn't last long. One of my rides stole what I had left. He gave me this scar." He fingered the scar on his face.

He shifted in his seat. "Please don't turn me in. I'll just keep on runnin.' Or maybe I'll just jump off of the bridge."

She leaned forward, afraid he might run, and touched his forearm. "Frederick, you didn't kill anyone. Your father recovered from his concussion. The fact is, he went to jail for beating your mother. He's still there. She must be frantic with worry about you. You must go back. Finish school. Please. I'll give you bus fare home."

He looked at her, eyes wide with surprise. "He isn't dead?" Relief washed over his face, and he dropped his head into his hands. "That's unbelievable. Though..." (his voice was bitter), "we'd all be better off if he was. Except me. I'd be in jail." He let out a long, weary sigh, shook his head. "I don't know what to do. I can't go back to that. My mom doesn't care. She drinks as bad as he did."

Violet was filled with pity for this boy. A wild idea occurred to her. She leaned forward, looking at him intently. "No one can blame you for protecting your mother. I'm sure the guilt has been eating at you all this time. You need to get on with your life and you deserve a much better one than you've had. I'll tell you what. If you come back, I'll let you live with me until you graduate, if your mother will allow it. I have a spare room. Would that work?"

He stared at her, shook his head. "That's awful nice of you. Why would you do that? Nobody else has ever wanted to help me."

"On the contrary. Your mother must care very much, as have many of your teachers, I'm sure. But I see a lot of potential in you, Frederick. I don't want to see that go to waste. I don't want you to ruin your life. I like you. I know you're a good person. You just need a chance."

His food arrived and she watched as he wolfed it down, hardly pausing for breath. Violet felt her eyes tearing up. The poor kid was starving. She leaned forward, she had to convince him.

"Frederick, I'm here on vacation. I'm obliged to finish it with my friend. But I want to help you. If I get you a bus ticket, will you go back home? Your mother would be so relieved. I'm sure that, for all her faults, she cares much more than you think. When we get back, I can ask her about changing your living arrangements, if you wish. Would you do that?"

He looked at her thoughtfully. "You'd do that for me?"

She nodded. He polished off his meal, as a look of hope softened his face. "Okay. I really appreciate it. I'd like to go home as long as my dad isn't there."

Violet smiled with relief. "Let's go to the department store down the street and get you some clean clothes. Then we'll head for the nearest bus station and get you a ticket."

He hung his head. "I—I guess I'm living pretty rough… I know I smell bad. I've been on the streets ever since I got here. I really appreciate your help."

She paid the bill and asked the waitress where the nearest bus station was. Luckily, it was just four blocks down the street. She spotted Betty, waiting discreetly outside. She explained to her what she was doing, and Betty came along with them. At the department store they spent nearly an hour getting the boy clean clothes from the skin out. They got to the bus depot, and Violet purchased a one-way ticket back to Bandon for the boy.

He would have a two-hour wait before his bus took off but at least he'd be warm and dry. She took forty dollars out of her purse and handed it to him. "This will give you money for food on the way. It's a long trip." She gestured toward the station's gift shop. "Perhaps you can pick up something to read over there. Will you be all right if we leave you here?"

Betty rummaged in her purse and handed him twenty dollars. "Take care of yourself, Frederick. Good luck to you." She gave him an encouraging smile.

He thanked her, ducking his head as his emotions played on his face. He turned to Violet. "I'll be okay. I sure do thank you. I hope you enjoy the rest of your vacation."

"I'll see you when we get home. Please take care of yourself." She patted him on the shoulder.

His lips curved in a faint smile. "I will." His eyes followed them out of the station.

Once outside, Betty remarked, "That poor boy will end up in prison or foster care, considering his home life. I hope his mother has quit drinking by the time he gets back but I doubt it."

Violet just muttered a non-committal "Hmmm."

Violet spent the rest of her trip wondering if he really did go home. After three more days of sightseeing, the friends bid Rose good-bye, with many thanks, and decided to head back to Oregon. When she got home, she plunked her suitcase on the floor, reached for the phone book, and called his mother. It turned out, Frederick had called her from Redding, told her he was all right. He wanted her to send him some things, some clothes and his birth certificate, which she did. Violet felt a twinge of relief. After all, she wasn't sure she could handle a teenage boy living in her house. She felt guilty about that. But he never came back to Bandon.

A year went by, and she kept herself busy with teaching and volunteering at church. One Saturday, during summer break, she felt the urge to write again, and got out her typewriter. She thought about a story she had been mulling over in her mind for some time. She began to type. She sat at the typewriter the rest of the day. When it got too dark to see, she realized that she needed to take a break and get something to eat.

She switched on the lights, went to the bathroom and then the kitchen, where she chugged down a huge glass of water. Grabbing the cottage cheese out of the refrigerator, she dumped a large helping into a bowl, then chopped an apple into it, then dropped a piece of bread into the toaster. She made a pot of coffee, quickly downed her repast, stretched, poured herself a large mug of coffee, and went back to the typewriter. For the next eight weeks she typed and re-typed like a woman possessed. She was forced to take occasional breaks to get groceries and met Betty for dinner out a couple of times. But she was always writing in her head.

Finally, after two months, she had a finished manuscript. It was a novel about a boy who grew up in a drunken, violent household, who killed his father and ran away. Eventually, he jumped off the Golden Gate Bridge. This time, she was sure she had a winner. The book had practically written itself. She made copies and sent them off to various publishers and agents. Three months later she received a call from an agency in New York. They liked her book. They wanted to sign her on and get it published. She was so thrilled that she danced all around her house, frightening the cats, who hid under her bed. She called Betty and told her they were going out to celebrate.

It took a while, but the book was finally published. It began to sell, and she went on a book tour. It didn't make the best-seller lists, but it sold a respectable amount. Her agent was urging her to write another. She retired from teaching and dedicated herself to writing.

One day, six years after the Frederick affair, as she thought of it, she received a large manila envelope in the mail. The return address was Arcata, California. In the envelope was a large picture of Frederick in a cap and gown, looking healthy and proud, holding a diploma. He was standing in front of a "Humboldt State University" sign. There was a pretty young woman by his side. On the back was a short note. "This wouldn't have happened if it weren't for you. Thank you for my life." That was all.

She stared at it a long time, as she sat in her rocking chair. Still smiling, she hugged the photo as she gently rocked. "Thank you, Frederick. Thank God," she whispered. And she laughed. This was her greatest achievement. If she never wrote another word, her life would be complete. She leaned back in her comfy chair and closed her eyes.

The gulls were back today, too.
A group of them had been hanging around
for the last two or three days.

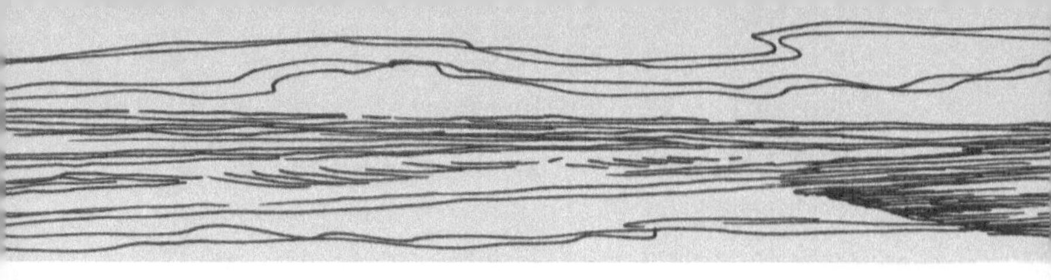

CHAPTER TWENTY

REENIE, HER LAST CHAPTER

THE SISTERS PACKED their bags and checked out of their room. On the way out of town, they made one last stop at the cemetery. As they made a final tour around their family and old acquaintances, they came upon Reenie's grave.

Allie pointed to the headstone. "Here's Reenie, Sophie. Everybody just loved her. She was such a fine person. She influenced a lot of people. I heard she had the biggest funeral ever seen in town. The paper ran a long obituary and people sent too many letters to the editor for him to print, telling of the good deeds and fun that Reenie had brought into their lives."

"I remember her. Mom was a good friend of hers. Now they're here together." The girls took a moment to read the headstone. "That's so appropriate, don't you think, Allie?"

She read aloud, "Reenie Adams, May 13, 1920-Feb. 6, 2006—A little woman with a giant heart. Beloved by all."

"It's perfect." Allie paused, thinking of the little sparkplug that had been Reenie. Finally, she turned away. "Well, let's take one last look at the harbor and then head out. I'm getting anxious to get back home, aren't you?"

They took in the view one more time, the harbor, the jetty, river and sea. Allie sighed. "You know, Sophie, I've decided to let go of all the hurts and bad memories. My tough senior year, the mean girls who tormented me, Ralph Maven who stood me up at the senior prom. I'm letting them go on out with the tide. I love this place, and I want to come back and just enjoy it."

Sophie nodded. "I think that's an excellent plan. I agree." They watched the scene for another few minutes, then finally tore themselves away and left the dead to commune with each other as they headed back to their everyday lives.

REENIE

Reenie looked up from the book in her lap and watched the waves crashing on the beach below her room. She had always been an enthusiastic reader, but lately she couldn't get interested in anything. The leaden skies, the gray sea, the whistling wind all made for a brooding landscape.

She was so glad of the sea view when she had been forced by a bad heart, at the age of eighty-six, to come to the nursing home. It was ever changing, always interesting, indeed mesmerizing, to watch. On stormy days she felt a flutter of excitement as she watched the huge rollers crash against the rocks. On calm days, it soothed her spirit. Today, it just depressed her. The fogbound bleakness of the scene seeped into her soul. The shore pines hunched their twisted limbs away from the shore, bracing themselves against the incessant wind.

The gulls were back today, too. A group of them had been hanging around for the last two or three days. They all hunkered down on the ground, facing the same direction. One of them stood on the railing outside her window. He seemed to be watching her, waiting for something. This was the third time she had noticed him. At least, she thought it was the same gull, but who could tell? It was getting creepy. She leaned forward and gazed at him. He cocked his head and stared back. Was he trying to tell her something?

"Gerry?" she whispered.

She pulled back and closed her eyes. If only she could just go to sleep and not wake up. What good did it do for her to be sitting around like this? What use was she to anyone? Almost everyone she had ever loved had moved away or was waiting for her in the graveyard.

One by one, she pictured the friends and family who had left her behind. Her husband, Gerald, the love of her life for forty-five years, was always first in her thoughts. Then, the son she adored, who had gone to Vietnam and not come back, her siblings and parents, and friends who had fallen by the wayside. All gone. Her equally adored daughters lived far away in Portland and Bend. Molly and Audrey came to visit as often as they could, only five or six times a year. They both called frequently, as did the grandchildren, but the telephone was cold comfort. And what was there to talk about? She was stuck here with nothing to do. Friends who came by occasionally provided some comfort, but she knew she was no longer a vital part of anyone's life.

She dozed. Her life visited her in dreams. She had worked hard from the time she was a child. She first earned money working in the hop fields around Yakima. The fields baked under the sun and the plants made her itch. But she sweated through the season every year from the time she was twelve until she finished high school. She used the money to pay her tuition to the St. Jude Academy, and for her school uniform, and for some other clothes and expenses she had.

Married at seventeen, with the Great Depression still devastating the country, she and Gerry moved to Oregon to try for a better life. The world went to war and she rejoiced when Gerry was rejected by the military because of his flat feet. As the war ended the depression, job opportunities opened.

Gerry found a job in a lumber mill for a while. Then babies came and he went to work in the woods for better pay. When a cable broke and whipped back, almost tearing him in two, he was hurt so badly that they had to move from the logging settlement back into Coos Bay, living with her grandparents for several months while he recovered. After that he tried various jobs until he got a job managing the feed/farm supply store for a steady paycheck. They settled in Bandon and she stayed home to care for the children.

Gerry suffered frequent pain from his past injuries, but he stoically went to work every day to support his family. Reenie carefully packed his lunch, kissed him goodbye, and watched as her handsome, dark-haired husband headed out to the car each morning. It always hurt her heart to see him painfully pull himself behind the wheel. But his family was the center of his life, and he would do whatever it took to support them. Reenie cooked and sewed and kept their little house clean. They had a small vegetable garden in back, which she enjoyed tending with the help of the three children. Those were sweet days, when the children were little.

However, once the children were all in school, Reenie

went to work again. There was the job at the laundry in Coquille, until it closed down. Then the job she hated most—picking crabmeat at the crab plant. Difficult, demanding and tedious, the sharp shells made mincemeat out of her hands. She only lasted at that one for two weeks. After that she tried clerking at one of the stores downtown. That was boring, so she moved to waitressing at a little hamburger joint at the top of the hill, right on the highway, called "Rob's." That was more fun. She got to schmooze with the locals who frequented the place. And she and Rob got along great.

One day, Rob called the restaurant just as Reenie was walking in the door. "Reenie, I'm too sick to come in this morning. You're goin' to haveta open the store today and do the cookin'."

"Are you crazy? I've never cooked in a restaurant before. I can't do that."

"Reenie, I'm countin' on you to come through for me here. I'm sick as a dog and can't come in. I'm sure you can handle it. You've seen me workin' in the kitchen. And you have Sally (the other current waitress) there to help you. It's just burgers and fries and coffee and ice cream. Everything's ready to go."

"I'll do my best. But if I can't keep up, I'll close the place until you're well enough to come back."

"We can't afford to shut down. I know you can do it. Thanks, Reenie." He hung up.

At first, Reenie panicked. What the Hell did she know about restaurant cooking? Then she thought about it, realized that the menu was pretty simple, and she had watched Rob working for several months. It couldn't be that hard, could it? Besides, she was a good cook. She bravely stepped into the kitchen and turned on the burners.

When Sally came in, she explained that the two of them were running the show. Sally's plucked eyebrows went up on her forehead. "Holy cow! This is crazy. Are you sure you can do it?"

"We'll see," was Reenie's grim reply. "Go ahead, open up."

So that was how she became the alternate cook. She loved that job, despite the fact that it was exhausting and hard on her hands and feet. The grease got in her hair, and it occasionally spattered and burned her skin, and the only breaks she got were when business was slow. But she got in on all the gossip the waitresses brought her. She joked with the staff and customers. She developed her own routine, and added some touches of her own, like creating rosemary fries, which became quite popular. And the high school kids drifted in and out. She adored the kids. She befriended the lonely ones and the strays, often those who needed a motherly friend. And her own children came in after school when finished with their activities, to have a snack and get a "mom hug" before they went on home. She loved to joke with everybody. Laughter filled the air when Reenie was around.

In 1969, the laughter stopped when she got the word that her son, Michael, had been killed in action in Vietnam. The pain of it never left her. Her beautiful, black-haired, six-foot, life-loving son, reduced to a corpse in a coffin.

Devastated, she left work. But, after three months of mourning, she knew that she needed to get back to where she was surrounded by people. Her girls were grown and gone. Gerry swallowed his misery and went back to work. She had to have a reason to get out of bed in the morning.

When she told Rob that she was ready to come back to work, he welcomed her with open arms. "Hell, yeah! The customers miss you and so do I. Haven't had a bit of rest since you left. Couldn't find any decent replacement."

It comforted her to see the kids coming in, and she learned how to go on with her life. She never lost interest in everything that went on in town. A natural gossip, she generally knew which way the wind blew throughout the population.

Gradually, she realized that she could smile and joke again, and put aside her pain while she was hustling around in the kitchen.

Their girls married and, to her utter delight, presented her with grandchildren. Eventually, there were five little ones to fill her heart to overflowing with love and pride. She visited them every chance she got, and their families traveled back home for vacations and school breaks. The grandchildren loved visiting them, loved playing on the beach. Reenie always made sure they had a good time when they came and fed them royally. After Reenie retired and the grandchildren were grown, they married and now there were three great-grandchildren, their pictures proudly displayed on her dresser.

Reenie, thinking about her busy, fulfilling past, glanced out her window again. There he was, that pesky sea gull. What did he want? A handout? She had nothing to give him. She leaned forward. "Shoo." The gull just stood there and stared. She decided to ignore him and turned away.

Again, her mind wandered back to the past. After Rob sold the cafe, she worked for the new owners for several years.

They expanded the place and hired more help. It wasn't the same atmosphere anymore, and as she aged, the work became too intense and exhausting, so she finally quit.

She did seasonal work in the box factory after that. It was a change of pace, and a chance to yak with the "girls." There was no pressure to rush, and her co-workers made it fun. The women there had their own stories, and they shared their lives with each other, laughter healing their hearts as they sorted through the boards that came by on the conveyor belt. They were not above practical jokes, and secretly enjoyed pulling pranks on the tolerant boss. He gave as good as he got, and Reenie frequently had a funny story to tell when she went home in the evening.

After she and Gerry sat down at the table and said grace, she would recount what had happened that day. "Sally put a live frog in Ralph's lunch box. You should have seen his face when he opened it. Then, when Myrtle complained that we never had enough toilet paper in the powder room, Ralph dumped a whole pallet of TP in front of the door. We had to clear away stacks of it before we could get in to relieve ourselves. One of the girls wet her pants and we couldn't stop laughing. I tell you, that place is crazy." Gerry would get a good laugh at the goings-on.

She had to quit working when Gerry developed lung cancer. It was the worst time of her life. She nursed him at home by herself until his final trip to the hospital.

Tears slipped down her cheeks as she thought about that horrible day. Now the one person who shared her pain at the terrible loss of their son was gone. Who else could know her as Gerry had? Who would hold her in the night and comfort her in her sorrow? Who else knew her entire life story?

The girls and their families came home for the funeral. They stayed as long as they could but then, too soon, had to get back to their own lives. They called frequently and tried to get her to move nearer to them. But she couldn't leave her friends and her church family. Who would tend the graves of her loved ones if she left? How could she live away from the sound of the sea? And she didn't want to leave the little house she had tended so carefully over the years. She stayed where she was.

It took her a long time to get used to the new rhythms of her life. She frequently visited her sister, Althea, who lived nearby with her husband. They grew closer than before. Up until her husband's death, the sisters had been busy with their own lives and hadn't spent a lot of time together. Now they called each other nearly every day, and often shopped together, and accompanied each other to church. They were pillars of the Altar Society.

When Althea died suddenly of a heart attack, it knocked the wind out of Reenie. Her last living sibling was gone. She was fully alone in the world, except for the children. They kept trying to talk her into moving near to them, but she couldn't bring herself to do it. And now it was too late. Her heart was failing, and the arthritis twisted her fingers and pained her body. She refused to "be a burden" to the children and went to the nursing home instead.

BRENDA WILSON

Brenda Wilson knocked softly on Reenie's door. She was a plump, cheery woman who looked younger than her fifty-three years, with sweet, soft brown eyes and a ready smile. She was proud of her practical nursing license and enjoyed working at the nursing home. And Reenie was her favorite patient. She loved Reenie.

When Brenda was ten years old, she came home from school one day to find her mother in another drunken stupor on the couch in the small trailer's living area. Brenda was hungry. She hadn't had anything to eat all day but stale cereal with water for breakfast, and a bread and "butter" sandwich for lunch. She went to the refrigerator in hopes that her mother had brought home some food. She stared at the empty shelves in despair. Nothing but ketchup and mustard and a stick of margarine. She considered eating the margarine, but the thought was repulsive. She rummaged through the chaos of the cupboards but there was only dried pasta and some canned sauces and beans. She considered the beans, but she really didn't like them. She shook her mother's arm, trying to wake her. The woman surfaced for a moment, opened bloodshot eyes halfway.

"Oh, hi Babe. Mama doesn't feel so good. Get y'self somethin' ta eat, okay?"

She turned away as Brenda watched her sink into the fog of oblivion. Brenda's heart sank.

She picked her mother's coat from off the floor and heard a clink in the pocket. She rummaged through both pockets and came up with 35¢ in her slightly grubby paw. She stared at the coins. She felt rich. She could buy a dozen candy bars. She could buy food.

She slipped quietly out of the trailer and trudged several blocks to Rob's. She hesitated at the door. She had never been to a restaurant by herself before. She was a little scared.

But the smell of hamburgers sizzling on the grill pulled her in without another thought. She stood at the counter staring up at the lady behind it. The lady was beautiful, with black-rimmed eyes and bright red lips. Her rust-red hair was piled in a stylish bouffant on top of her head. She looked at Brenda and smiled kindly.

"Is there somethin' I can do for you, Hon?"

Brenda held out her hand with the change and whispered, "What can I get for this?"

The lady bent down and looked at her hand. "Well, Honey, you can get a ice cream cone."

"Can I get a hamburger?"

"I'm afraid you'd need fifteen more cents to get that."

Suddenly a short older lady, with black hair stuffed in a hairnet, wearing a stained white apron, was standing at the lady's elbow. "What's your name, Sweetie?"

Brenda ducked her head and softly said, "Brenda."

The black-haired lady looked at the skinny, pale kid with the bare legs and no socks, wearing a tattered windbreaker jacket, and smiled. "Well, you know what, Brenda? It just so happens that we're havin' a special today. For one quarter and a dime you can get a milkshake, a hamburger and French fries. How does that sound?"

Brenda saw the red-haired lady look at the small lady with a funny expression, sort of a half-frown and half-smile at the same time. She ignored that and grinned broadly at the small lady. "I'd love that."

So, she hopped up on a stool at the counter and got the best meal she could remember and became friends for life with Reenie Adams.

Brenda peeked into Reenie's room. Reenie was slumped

in her rocker, her head hanging. Brenda felt a pang of anxiety. Was Reenie gone? She stepped into the room and examined Reenie more closely. She was breathing. Brenda let out her breath and spoke softly.

"Reenie. Reenie. It's time to eat." She gently shook the old lady's shoulder.

Reenie opened her eyes and smiled. "Oh, Brenda, I was with my Gerry. He was so happy to see me. I didn't want to wake up."

Brenda smiled back. "Well, Reenie, why don't you come have some dinner and then you can go to bed and dream about him all night."

Reenie reached up and touched her cheek. "You were always such a sweet girl. You take such good care of me. I'm really not hungry. Can I just have a bite here in my room?"

"Don't you want to join the others? It's not like you not to socialize."

"I'm just so tired. I don't want to move. I don't want to leave Gerry."

Brenda was worried. It wasn't like Reenie to be depressed. She was always so happy to see people and visit. She never complained about her aches and pain, even though Brenda knew she must suffer a lot from the arthritis. She gently warmed Reenie's tiny, gnarled hand in her two warm ones.

"If I bring you a tray, will you promise me you'll eat?"

A small smile played on Reenies' lips and she nodded. "Yes ma'am."

Brenda looked at her closely, then left the room. She could feel that Reenie was withdrawing, just waiting for the end. She didn't want to lose her. They had been friends for so long. She would miss her terribly, as would half the town.

She went to the kitchen and filled a plate for Reenie, trying to select things that she knew her friend liked, in small portions so as not to overwhelm her. Reenie ate so little; she wanted the food to tempt her. It was as if Reenie wanted to just fade out of existence.

Brenda hurried back to the room. Reenie was sitting in the same place, rosary in hand. It was never far from her reach. She looked up as Brenda came in. "Thank you so much, Sweetie. You're so good to me."

"Nothin's too good for you, Reenie. You saved my bacon more than once and I'll never forget it. Now, please eat a nice dinner. Then, if you want, I'll help you bathe and tuck you into bed and you can watch a little TV before you go to sleep. Laurence Welk's on tonight, remember."

"Oh, I do love him. He has the best music."

"I have to hustle out and help with people in the dining room. I'll be back in about an hour. Now, you eat a nice dinner, hear?"

"Yes ma'am. Whatever you say."

Later that evening, Brenda helped Reenie get cleaned up and into her warm flannel nightgown and tucked her into bed. She turned on the television making sure Reenie could see the screen. She would come back later and turn it off before she went home. She picked up the food tray. It looked like a sparrow had pecked at it. She knew it would do no good to urge her patient to eat more.

As she turned to leave the room, Reenie stopped her with a question. "Brenda, have you seen the gulls hanging around outside my window?"

"I did notice that one on the sill. Looked like he was

wanting to come in. Those things creep me out sometimes."

"I can't help but feel they're waiting for something. Maybe waiting for me to die."

Brenda gasped. "Whatever would make you think such a thing? I'm sure what they're waiting for is someone to throw them some bread. Nothing more than that. You're scaring me, Reenie."

"I'm sorry, Honey. Don't let me get you down. Sometimes I have too much imagination."

"I think maybe you do. Anyway, you relax and enjoy your program. No gulls are going to get in here."

"Okay, Honey. I'll say goodnight now."

"Good night, Reenie. I'll check in on you later." She walked out the door.

When she got home, her husband Phil had warmed up the casserole she had left in the refrigerator for her family. They ate together, then cleaned up what was left of the mess and relaxed in front of the TV for a while. They both turned in at ten o'clock. That was when they did their real talking. Snuggled in bed, arms around each other, they had their most meaningful conversations.

"You know, Phil, I'm worried about Reenie. She seems to just be giving up on life. It's so sad. I hate to think of losing her. She's been such a big influence in my life. Practically kept me alive when I was growing up. She's been more like a mother to me than my own ever was."

"Well, Honey, she's really old. People just get tired and want to get it over with when they get that old. Maybe it'd be better for her to just let go."

"But I'd miss her so much. I must have been thirteen before I realized that she was feedin' me out of her own pocket. All that time, I thought they were running 'specials.' I can never repay her for all her kindness. She'd talk to me and counsel me. I'm sure, if it weren't for her, I'd have dropped out of high school. I owe her a lot."

"Lovie, I know you hate to talk about your past, but don't you think it'd be good to tell her how you feel before she dies? It'd make her feel real good. Maybe even perk her up a bit."

"Y'know what? That's a good idea. I never have really told her how much she's meant to me. It's time I did. I want her to live to be a hundred. We'll have a big party and invite the whole town."

She could see his white teeth grinning in the dark as he tightened his grip around her. "You're pretty special too, you know that?" He sat up. "Come on, let me give you a back rub. It'll help you relax. Then I'll show you how much you mean to me."

The next day Brenda checked in and went to Reenie's room. She was lying in her bed, eyes closed. Brenda tiptoed up to the bed and looked closely at Reenie. She was smiling slightly. Her rosary was wrapped around her hand. She wasn't breathing. She was gone. Brenda felt her cold wrist, trying to find a pulse. There was none.

Tears slid down Brenda's cheeks. "Reenie, you left before I could tell you how much you meant to me. You knew, I'm sure. And I have such a hard time talking about my feelings with anybody. But I should have told you that you probably saved my life. You fed me, and listened to me, and helped me in so many ways."

She paused, stifled a sob. "You even gave me clothes. Remember that beautiful coat you gave me when I was twelve? And the shoes you gave me when I didn't have decent ones to wear to school? You kept me goin', Reenie. You gave me hope and showed me what love was." The words tumbled out over the painful lump in her throat. "Thank you, Reenie. I love you. I wish you didn't have to leave. You'll be missed by everybody." She gently pulled the covers up over the cold shoulders. Reenie was always cold lately, it seemed. Brenda straightened up and looked at Reenie one last time. She'd better notify the head nurse. As she turned to go, she glanced out the window. The gulls were gone.

THE END

We hope you've enjoyed *Cast By The Sea*.

What was your favorite moment in the book?

Who was your favorite character?

Would you recommend this
book to others?

Please post reviews, however brief to
your favorite places such as Goodreads,
online book clubs, and social pages.

You may also contact the author at:
theresavwrites.com

Thank you for your support and for being our reader!

ABOUT THE AUTHOR

THERESA VERBOORT was born in Coos Bay, Oregon, and grew up in the southwestern coast during the 50s. Her first novel, *The Communing Tree*, inspired by the Kalmiopsis Wilderness of Oregon, won the prestigious WILLA Literary Award for best young adult fiction of 2019. *A Sapling Grows*, the sequel, was published in 2023. This third book, *Cast by the Sea*, takes place in her hometown, Bandon, Oregon. The fictitious cast of characters, in a beautiful, coastal setting, will win your heart.

—

If you would like to receive notifications from the author and blog post updates now and then, please subscribe to Theresa's mailing list at www.theresavwrites.com